STO

D1062773

LEETE'S ISLAND ADVENTURE

LEETE'S
ISLAND
ADVENTURE

Dorothy M. Broderick

j B 7826 l

PRENTICE-HALL, INC.   Englewood Cliffs, N. J.

Library of Congress Catalog Card Number: 62-11364

COPYRIGHT UNDER INTERNATIONAL AND PAN-AMERICAN
COPYRIGHT CONVENTION

© 1962 by Prentice-Hall, Inc., Englewood Cliffs, N. J.
All rights reserved, including the right to reproduce this book, or any
portions thereof, in any form, except for the inclusion of brief quotations
in a review. Printed in the United States of America.

52719-J

To
Shirley Frazier,
teacher and friend

CO. SCHOOLS
C544763

AUTHOR'S NOTE

The characters and events portrayed are
entirely imaginary and any resemblance to
actual people, living or dead, is coincidental.
However, the Island is real and the people
who live on it in real life are as wonderful as
I hope you find the fictional ones.

CONTENTS

DEPARTURE

"THERE IS ABSOLUTELY NO reason for this chaos!" shouted Mr. Barker. "We've been organized and ready to go for two weeks," he muttered to himself.

The chaos continued unabated and Mr. Barker might just as well have shouted his words into the center of a cyclone for all the good they did him. He paced the hall-way, which ran the length of the apartment, looking into each room of the six-room apartment. The one at the end of the hall contained his son, Buddy, who was in the process of shouting, "Mom, I can't find my new baseball glove."

"It's already packed," said Mr. Barker. "Now, will you take that howling demon down and get him settled in the car?"

"Sure, Dad," said Buddy. The "howling demon" referred to a small black, white and brown mongrel dog tied to the front doorknob. Baroque was not used to being restrained and the whole sixth floor of the apartment house was being kept informed of the indignity to which he was being subjected.

"What's the matter, fellow? Don't like being tied up,

9

do you? Well, you'll soon be running free, so relax." Buddy slipped the loop of the leash off the knob and Baroque calmed down. Together they stepped into the outer hallway and patiently waited for the slow-moving, less-than-reliable, elevator.

"Did someone call me?" asked Mrs. Barker, emerging from the kitchen.

"Only your son. Looking for the baseball glove he packed a week ago. Honestly, Mary, if we don't leave soon, I'll have a nervous breakdown."

"Nonsense, Bill. It's not any worse than other years," his wife said.

"I suppose not, but I keep thinking the older the kids get, the easier it should be," he said.

"Children don't get better or worse, dear, only different," she said, and Mr. Barker smiled.

"Well, are you, at least, ready to go?" he asked.

"Yes, dear. I was just checking to be sure the kitchen was clean."

"It was five years ago we left the coffee pot," Mr. Barker said. "We haven't done it since and I don't know why you worry so." Mr. Barker was referring to the time Mrs. Barker had forgotten to wash out the coffee pot and had returned to find the coffee had turned to a horrible green mold. She had thrown the pot out despite assurances from Mr. Barker that all it needed was a good scouring.

"I know, Bill, but last year we left Baroque's dish with half a can of dog food in it. I have visions of the apartment being over-run by green monsters while we're away."

"All right, Mary. Do you think we can get the rest of

3 1833 04380 6642

our home-grown menagerie on the road?" Mr. Barker walked into the living room and said, "Linda, are you coming with us, or not?"

"Do I have a choice?" she asked, her words muffled because her face was half under the couch.

"What did you say?" Mr. Barker asked.

"I said, Rococo won't come out from under the couch," Linda replied, coming up for air. She returned to the task at hand, saying quietly, "Come on, Roc. Nobody's going to hurt you. That's a boy, come on."

Rococo, a tabby tomcat, measuring twenty-two inches from the tip of his nose to the beginning of his tail, looked at Linda and cautiously backed further away. He might not understand the words, but he recognized the tone of voice as one that had lured him into miserable situations in the past. He had fallen for it once and ended up in the bathtub; a second time it had resulted in having his nails clipped. He wasn't having any more of that particular voice.

Mr. Barker paced the living room. "Get the broom and knock him out from under," he said. He turned away as Linda said, "Oh, Dad!" He looked out the window at a barge floating down the Hudson River. It was a calming view under most circumstances, but getting a family on the road wasn't one of them.

"Why don't you go down and check the car, Bill?" Mrs. Barker asked. "We'll be with you in a minute."

"A minute! We'll be lucky if we get there before Labor Day at this rate," he said, but he went.

"Linda, try this," Mrs. Barker said, handing her a piece of string.

Linda pulled the string slowly back and forth in front

of the couch. It seemed ages before Roc made his first tentative gesture. He moved his head back and forth like a spectator at a tennis match; then he crouched, gave a wiggle and pounced.

A moment later Rococo found himself locked into the carrying case and probably wondering why he always fell for that trick. The problem was, of course, that it wasn't always a trick. Sometimes Linda just wanted to play. That was what made it so difficult.

"You're a mess," Mrs. Barker said, looking at the streaks of dirt on Linda's face, "but no one's going to see you so I guess it's all right."

The carrying case, bought when Rococo was young, was too small for him to ride in comfortably and once the car was moving, Linda opened the case and let him out. As soon as the case was open, he began to howl. His tongue hung out, his eyes bulged and his sides heaved as though about to burst. It would be an understatement, Linda thought, to say that Roc was not fond of riding in automobiles.

"If that cat howls all the way, I swear I'll drown him when we get there," Mr. Barker said.

"Really, Dad," Linda replied, "your threats would have much more force if you didn't always resort to hyperbole."

"That's a nice word," Mr. Barker said, suppressing a smile. "Where did you find it?"

"In a book," Linda answered easily.

Traffic was heavy and it took forty minutes from the time they left the apartment until they crossed the White-stone Bridge. "Seems strange, doesn't it, that in less than an hour and a half we'll cover seventy-five miles while it takes forty minutes to cover ten," Mr. Barker noted. No one paid attention to the remark since he always made it. It fell into the same category as complaints about it taking an hour to fly from Boston to New York but an hour and a half to get from the airport to home.

Rococo had settled down a bit but he still looked as though a heart attack were imminent. At least the howling had stopped. Baroque lay quietly on the floor at Buddy's feet, thoroughly contented with life.

"It's going to be nice to see everyone again," Mrs. Barker said.

"Yes, they're a nice crew," Mr. Barker agreed.

Linda listened half-heartedly as her mother talked on about how pleasant it would be to see the "regulars" again. As long as Linda could remember, which was about twelve of her fifteen years, they had spent their summers on Leete's Island. It had been fun, but each year it seemed to become less so.

The Island was a small, privately-owned piece of land off the Connecticut coast in Long Island Sound. It was difficult for strangers to see at first glance that it was an island since it lay close to the mainland and was approached by car. It was less difficult to see when a hurricane brought a tidal wave that covered the road.

Mrs. Barker was discussing the Winstands, the Corwins, and the Babcocks now. They were all nice people, Linda had to admit, but none of them had children her age. Particularly, to be blunt about it, she thought, there aren't any boys on Leete's Island. And there comes a time in a girl's life when swimming, boating, sleeping out under the stars, and beach cookouts simply aren't enough. What was the sense of seeing every star in the sky when the only person who looked at them with you was your twelve-year-old brother?

"Harry should have a few tales to tell," Mr. Barker said. That was Harry Babcock who had spent the previous year in Egypt teaching chemistry at the University of Cairo. Linda decided it was no use conjuring up an imaginary boy who would appear out of nowhere and make the summer complete, so she joined the conversation.

"If I'd been Mr. Babcock, I wouldn't have gone to Egypt," she announced.

"And why not?" her father asked, and immediately began to regret it. It was time he stopped playing straight man for Linda.

"Well, not unless they made a few concessions," Linda said. "I'd have told them, 'I'll come if you let the Israeli ships through the Suez Canal.'"

Mr. Barker choked on his cigarette smoke and Mrs. Barker coughed into her handkerchief. "Do you think that would have solved the problem?" her father asked.

"Perhaps not," Linda admitted, "but it would have let them know I didn't approve. After all, Dad, there is such a thing as morality in world affairs."

"I do believe you've over-simplified a very complex situation," Mr. Barker said. "I suppose you've also mapped out a plan for settling the differences between the East and West."

"As a matter of fact. . ." Linda began.

"Never mind," her father said. "Don't tell me. I don't think I can drive and listen to you solve the world's problems at the same time."

"Yeah," Buddy chimed in, "you'll give Dad a trauma."

"Mary, I must have been a very retarded twelve-year-old," Mr. Barker said. "I don't believe I knew what a trauma was at that age. By the way, Buddy, do you know what the word means?"

"Sure. That's what happens when a kid who's old enough to have one asks his father for an outboard motor for his boat and is turned down." Buddy grinned at Linda as if to say, I knew I could work that in if I tried hard enough.

"I absolutely give up," Mr. Barker moaned.

"Traffic's picking up," Mrs. Barker said, changing the subject with her usual ease.

"We'll lose most of it in another two miles. There's a toll coming up and the smart boys will get off and waste a half hour and a gallon of gas to avoid spending the quarter," Mr. Barker said.

People were silly, Linda thought. She leaned back and closed her eyes. The thruway was a magnificent road, but it certainly did not provide anything to look at except factories and swamps. It probably wouldn't help, but she decided to dream anyway.

Dreaming had one big drawback, she realized. She did not really know enough about boys even to conjure up one. Of course, she knew she didn't want one like Jimmy Sampson who sat behind her in history class and thought it great fun to drop paper clips down her back. An older boy with more sense, she thought. At least sixteen; seventeen would be ideal. In a pinch, she admitted reluctantly, he could even be her age, but that was a last resort.

He didn't have to be too tall; anywhere from 5'8" would do. Tall, willowy women were attractive, but they had trouble finding men, she thought, and was grateful to be 5'4". Buddy was going to be the big one in the Barker family and that was all right with her. As for the color of her dream-boy's hair and eyes, she had no opinion. It was silly to set up standards when she was willing to take what—who—came along.

In the opposite corner, Buddy thought about motors. He had read every book on small boats in the library. He knew how to adjust a carburetor and clean spark plugs. He knew just about all there was to owning a motor boat except how to convince Dad to buy him one.

ARRIVAL

THE ARRIVAL WAS EVEN MORE hectic than the departure. Mr. Barker had not braked the car to a full stop when Baroque, spying a baby cottontail in the high grass, leaped through the open car window and began a loud chase.

Rococo, after two hours of riding, was determined not to be exposed to any new dangers and gripped the upholstery with all twenty of his claws. Linda finally dislodged him from his terrified grip but as she headed for the open door of the cottage Roc leaped from her arms and slipped under the house.

"Leave him be," Mrs. Barker said. "He needs time to get used to the place and at least he's out from under foot for a while."

Linda got up from her prone position and brushed the cobwebs from her face. It seemed to her that in the ten months she had owned Rococo, she had spent at least five of them on the floor.

For the next half-hour the four of them worked carrying loads of equipment from the station wagon. It was piled, not too neatly, Mrs. Barker noted, on the porch.

"I'll open up," Buddy said, and proceeded to climb on a chair and swing the porch windows up to the ceiling and hook them. The porch was protected by a canopy and no rain ever penetrated its sanctity. The other windows in the house pushed out from the bottom and also provided protection from rain.

"Goodness, Buddy," Mrs. Barker said, "you've grown a foot since last year."

"Yeah, I couldn't reach the hooks last year, could I?" he asked with a glow in his eyes.

"Do we start with an open or closed house?" Mr. Barker asked.

"Open, I think, dear," Mrs. Barker answered. "It will save footsteps and I'm sure we would all like to get this over with as soon as possible."

"Boy, I want to go swimming," Buddy announced.

"I imagine the water's too cold," his father said.

Buddy, ignoring his father's words, said, "Can I roll the walls up?" It was not a difficult job, but it had its fascination and Buddy proudly pushed a lever on the control board and watched the partition between the living room and the west bedroom roll up like an overhead garage door and lodge safely in a set of grooves in the ceiling. He pushed a second lever and the wall between the living room and the east bedroom disappeared overhead.

Mr. Barker stood and watched the procedure. "Best idea I ever had," he said proudly.

"It was, indeed," his wife agreed. "Buddy," she asked, "will you check the level in the rain barrels?"

"Right, Mom." A few seconds later he was back, slamming the screen door behind him. "Full to the brim. Want me and Dad to go fill the bottles?"

"That would be nice," his mother said. She knew, however, from past experience that the joy of carting ten five gallon jugs of water up the hill, car or no car, would soon wear off.

"If *only* we had our own well," she said.

"It would cost more to sink a well through this rock than it cost to build the cottage in the first place," Mr. Barker said.

"I know, Bill. I'm just dreaming. You shouldn't take me seriously," Mrs. Barker said. "Now, why don't you go for the water and Linda and I will get lunch ready. I think we're all in need of some nourishment."

Lunch over, the unpacking continued, but the initial enthusiasm had lost its force. When Buddy accidentally hit Linda on the leg with a suitcase, she growled, "Why don't you look where you're going, stupe?"

"And what are you doing in the middle of the room?" he snapped back.

"Why don't you two go sit on the beach?" Mrs. Barker suggested. "It's probably much too cold to go swimming, but you might wade around or something."

"An excellent idea," said Mr. Barker. "Run off, you two. Mother and I will take a quick trip into town and buy a little food while you're gone."

"I better get Rococo and put him in the house," Linda said. "I don't want him running away or meeting a strange dog while no one's around."

Buddy followed her out the door and watched her try to lure Roc into the open. Rococo's eyes were dilated with fear and he looked at Linda as though he had never seen her before. None of the usual tricks caused so much as a twitch of his whiskers.

"He's too scared to move," Buddy said. "Want me to crawl in and hand him out to you?"

"Thanks, Buddy. But be careful. He scratches when he's frightened."

With Rococo safely in the house, Buddy and Linda headed for the beach. It was too early in the season for many people to be around and the walk down the hill was a peaceful one. A rabbit looked out at them from the high grass, his big brown eyes seeming to take up his whole head.

"Looks like Little Georgie, doesn't he?" asked Linda.

"Uh-huh," Buddy answered. "Gee, I bet we could have our own Rabbit Hill if it weren't for all the pets people have."

"I'm afraid I'd want a selected group, though," Linda said. "I don't mind reading about things like skunks, but I sure don't want one sitting on our front step."

"Hey, can't you see that? One good spray and you'd be out of circulation for weeks. We'd probably have to leave your food on the picnic table and you could pick it up when the wind was blowing away from the house."

"You're a real sweet kid," Linda said.

Buddy, never one to prolong a conversation, ran ahead, shouting, "I'm going to look in the mailbox."

It's too early for mail, Linda thought, but at least it gives him something to do. The excitement of arriving had left her tired and feeling just this side of sorry for herself. Buddy was all right, really. And she had a good set of parents, but the summer loomed long and lonely. Just one boy, she thought. He didn't have to be handsome and own a boat or anything like that. He didn't even need to be the romantic type. Just someone to talk to and smile at.

Then, reaching the zenith of desperation, she thought, even a girl my own age would be some help.

"Hey, there's a big fat letter for Mr. Babcock," Buddy announced as he rejoined her. "I think I'll take it up to him on our way back."

"You know better than that, Buddy. Dad's told you a thousand times you're to leave other people's mail alone. Want the FBI looking for you?"

"You're such a dope, Linda. It wouldn't be the FBI. It would be the Postal Inspectors. But anyway, it might be fun. At least it wouldn't be the same old thing."

"Do you get bored, too?" Linda asked, but Buddy was running ahead again.

"Look, there's a convention of crabs," he shouted.

Linda kicked off her moccasins and walked to the water's edge where seven horseshoe crabs lay piled together. "Here comes another one," she said.

"Boy, they must have a built-in radar system or something," Buddy said. "I wonder if I were ship-wrecked on a desert island if I'd get hungry enough to eat one of those monsters. They're sure ugly."

"If you got hungry enough, you'd eat anything," Linda said. It amazed her, when she stopped to think about it, that Buddy's day dreams always took him to the moon or a desert island or involved him in a scrape with the FBI, while all she wanted was a peaceful, orderly life, with one boy to talk to.

"Jeepers, Dad was right. This water's cold," Buddy said. He did not, however, retreat from the icy grip.

Linda put one foot in up to the ankle and said, "A few minutes in that and Leete's Island would have its own Abominable Snowman."

"What's that?"

"Oh, a figure that mountain climbers see in the Himalayas. He's like a ghost or something. Some people really think he's alive and they try all kinds of tricks to find him."

"Sounds like the headless horseman kind of stuff. Maybe if I put on my white sailing pants and shirt and slipped around in the moonlight, we could get people to thinking the Island had a ghost. Wouldn't that be fun?"

"Swell fun!" Linda said. "They'd either find you out and lock you up as the nut you are, or else you'd scare everyone away and leave the Island lonelier than ever."

Linda walked back to where she had dropped her towel and lay face down under the bright sun. It was warm and the heat felt good on her bare back. She felt the drops of perspiration beginning to form and she wished, for just a passing second, that she could remember what it was she had learned in science class about the water taking longer to heat up than the earth but staying warm longer in the fall. There were just too many things to know in this world, she thought, and gave it all up. A little nap would be nice.

THE MISSING

MAILBOX

THE VACATION BEGAN SLOWLY and Linda contented herself with lying in the sun and occasionally dipping a toe into the water. She was the only member of the family without a consuming passion, and it bothered her.

Every morning her mother whipped through breakfast and the dishes so she could work in her herb garden. There were squeals of delight on Tuesday morning when she found the red mullein and the white digitalis had bloomed overnight. Combined with the purple sage, the herb garden was a thing of beauty. A few of the more advanced plants found their way into the dinner salad and the family had not yet decided whether it was better to know or be in ignorance of what they were eating.

Linda's father was even less communicative. After breakfast he would settle himself at the drafting table to work on the plans he would submit in the fall to an international architectural competition for the best design of a jet airport. There were no squeals of delight from Dad's corner and the occasional words he did mutter were not for Linda's ears.

Even Buddy worked happily scraping the old paint off his boat so he could get it into the water by the July 4th weekend. Motor or no, the boat had to be in top shape and Buddy worked diligently.

The closest Linda came to having an activity was cat-watching while Rococo bird-watched. Rococo had been raised in an apartment and to him the outside world consisted of the Hudson River as seen from six stories up. Now he found himself forced to lead an outdoor life. The first day he refused to stand up while outside and crawled on his stomach all over the yard. The second day he discovered, while instinctively leaping at a passing butterfly, that his feet functioned on grass as well as on floors. Linda turned away each time he snagged a butterfly, which was quite often. He did not, however, understand why the birds stayed so far away.

Wednesday started as usual. Mrs. Barker began by calling them all to admire her flax which was a half-inch out of the ground.

"I guess I'd better order that spinning wheel any day now," Mr. Barker said.

"Say, Mom, maybe you can enter hand-woven linens in the fair this year," Buddy exclaimed.

"You're all so funny," Mrs. Barker said, taking a playful swing at Buddy.

It was a routine beginning to a routine day. Linda, her chores over, took her book and stretched out in the lawn chair. She read for half an hour, but, as good as the book was, it did not satisfy her restless mood. It was a sign of desperation when she sauntered around the corner of the house and said, "Want me to help you?"

Buddy looked up as though seeing a total stranger appear out of nowhere. "Do I know you? Of course, the Abominable Snowman of Leete's Island." He continued to stare at her and finally said, "Are you kidding?"

"Look, I offered to help. If you don't want me to, say so," Linda replied.

"Wait a minute. Don't get huffy! Sure I want your help," Buddy said.

"So what do I do?" Linda asked.

Buddy picked up a block of wood and wrapped a piece of heavy sandpaper around it. "All you do is rub," he said.

Linda rubbed patiently for the better part of an hour, then she went to the refrigerator and brought back two glasses of milk and two bananas. "Coffee break," she announced.

"I must say this good country air is doing things for you," Buddy said, his voice filled with appreciation for this new sister of his. Between bites, he added, "Do you think there's any chance Dad will change his mind about buying me a motor?"

"I doubt it, Buddy. I've never yet seen Dad go back on a major decision. Remember that time he told me I could not have a pair of high heels and wouldn't let me buy them even when I saved up my own money?"

"Do I remember! When you called him the meanest father in the Western Hemisphere I thought you were going to end up in the river."

"At least I've never made that mistake again. And I wouldn't advise you to try it, not if you value your hide," Linda said. "You know, Buddy, it takes an awful long time to get used to parents. You'd think Dad would slip up once in a while, wouldn't you?"

"Yeah, and I keep thinking this might be it. After all,

I only want a little motor. Three horsepower is all the pram would take and still float. I can just see it. Give the string a pull, the motor goes putt-putt and off I go with no strain, no pain. What a life!"

"You're just lazy, Buddy. Think of all the muscles you'll get by rowing. When you go out for football in a couple of years, you'll be in shape."

Buddy, choosing to ignore that consolation, returned to scraping and Linda took the glasses into the kitchen. When she returned she asked, "What are you going to name it this year?" She was determined to stay off the subject of motors if at all possible.

"I don't know, but I'd better think of something quick before Dad sticks her with one of his famous monikers. Do you know, Linda, I still shudder when I think he wanted to name me Gropius. Can you imagine what that would have done to my life?"

"I guess I should be grateful that there aren't any famous women architects," Linda said.

"Maybe I'll call her 'Muscle Builder' since that's what she's destined to be," Buddy said after a long silence.

"The tide's about up. Want to go for a swim before lunch?" Linda asked. Her hands were sore from gripping the sandpaper block and her arms ached, but she hated to admit it.

"I'm with you," Buddy said eagerly.

Half way down the hill, Linda's leisurely pace became too much for Buddy and he took off with a leap, shouting over his shoulder, "I'll see you on the rocks."

Linda had reached the turn in the road that brought her to the edge of the beach when Buddy reappeared.

"Hey, guess what? Someone's swiped the A through C mailbox."

"The heat's got you. Who'd want to steal a mailbox?"

"How do I know? I'm just giving you the facts. The mailbox is gone so somebody must've swiped it," Buddy said.

"It probably needed fixing and Mr. Leete took it to be repaired," Linda said.

"It was all right the other day," Buddy replied. "Say, I'll bet it has something to do with that big letter for Mr. Babcock. Maybe he got mixed up in something over in Egypt and they're after him."

"Who's after him? Honestly, Buddy, sometimes you're the limit."

"Well. . . the Communists, maybe. I've been reading in *Time* that they're all over Egypt."

"You're some detective," Linda said. "So the Communists don't want Mr. Babcock to get a letter. They could come along, open the box, take out the letter and be gone. But, no, not according to Buddy Barker. It would be easier to rip a huge mailbox from a post than to slide one small letter into their pockets. Brother, you need a rest."

"Oh, all right, Miss Smarty," Buddy said. He dropped his towel and shirt on the rocks and dejectedly headed for the water.

The Island was a series of coves, each separated from the other by a rocky projection. It was on the rocks that Linda decided to stretch out. Years of being exposed to the rain and ocean had smoothed the rocks to the point where even lying on them was comfortable. I'll go in, Linda thought, but later after I've had time to prepare myself for hitting the icy water. I do wish Buddy wouldn't go off on tangents like that, she added.

"I know why," Buddy announced as he crawled out of the water.

"Why what?"

"Why they took the whole box, stupe. That way nobody knows for sure who they're after. It might be anyone named A, B or C. Why, it might even be us!"

Linda shook her head slowly and asked, "Did you ever read *Tom Sawyer*?"

"Tried it last year, but I didn't get too far. What's that got to do with this?"

"You remind me a little of Tom, except for one important difference. He used to go around playing at being a pirate, or a robber, or Robin Hood. But he, at least I think so, always knew he was pretending. You worry me."

Buddy glared down at her, then shook his wet hair violently. The cold drops splattered over Linda's warm body but before she could retaliate, Buddy was back in the water.

"Just you wait!" she called after him. The phrase was from her favorite song in *My Fair Lady* and she sang softly to herself: "Just you wait, 'enry 'iggins, just you wait!" Oh, how she sympathized with Eliza Doolittle and her trials with stupid men.

The afternoon was peaceful. Buddy finished the scraping job and began caulking the seams of the boat; Mom was taking an afternoon nap; and Dad was out on one of his "inspiration walks." Linda moved the lawn chair to the shade and stretched out to watch Rococo who was crouched under a low hanging branch with about three leaves on it, in the mistaken notion that the birds could not see him. He never flicked his tail when the catbird flew to the branch above and sat calling, "cat, cat, cat," until Linda wanted to throw a rock at him.

"Oh, Roc, you're so stupid," Linda said lovingly.

Rococo looked up at her as if to say, You can't see me; I'm hiding, so please don't talk to me.

"Poor thing, you really think they can't see you, don't you?" Linda asked. She received no answer.

In spite of the diversionary activities, Linda found to her annoyance that an unwelcome thought kept passing through her mind when she wasn't on guard. The thought was a question: actually, who *would* want to steal a mailbox?

She stood up and walked over to watch Buddy work. She did it casually, as though she were just passing by and had stopped to look. With determination, she forced herself to say, "Buddy, maybe one of the kids took it." She spoke softly so Mom wouldn't be disturbed.

"So, it's got you?" he gloated.

"Shh, you'll wake Mom," Linda said.

Buddy left off caulking and beckoned her to follow him. They moved away from the house to the picnic bench out back. Safely away from the house, Buddy continued his reply. "Listen, Linda, you know no kid would do it. Why, even that louse Kenny Mason didn't tamper with mail, and there wasn't much he didn't do."

"I suppose you're right," Linda admitted, "but even if you are, what can we do about it?"

"There's only one thing we can do; keep our eyes and ears open and see what happens," Buddy said.

"You think something is going to happen?"

"Sure. It has to, Linda. The stage is all set and all we have to do is be ready for our next clue."

"Oh, this is silly," Linda said, ashamed at having thought seriously about such a ridiculous situation.

"Is it?" Buddy asked. He went back to his boat, leaving Linda to her thoughts.

LIFE PICKS UP

ALL DAY THURSDAY AND PART of Friday morning it rained, but by mid-afternoon the sun was shining, as though in welcome for the new arrivals. Friday was July first and the summer began officially.

Mr. and Mrs. Barker sat on the porch and waved and called out greetings to the new arrivals as they drove slowly up the hill to their cottages. The quiet was broken by dogs barking, children crying, and the shouts of "Hold the door open," or "Put it there," as the unpacking and settling in began.

Saturday was reunion day and the Winstands, Corwins and Babcocks gathered at the Barker home for hot dogs cooked over a charcoal fire and talk of happenings over the long winter. Since none of the Barkers' close friends had children of Linda's or Buddy's age, the two slipped away after lunch to the beach.

Linda was half-way down the hill when she remembered her book. She never went to the beach without one even though she hardly ever got to read it. She used it as camouflage to avoid looking directly at the goings-on. It was a trick she had learned from her mother who never

31

seemed to be looking at anything, yet managed to see all.

"I'll see you there," she told Buddy and turned back.

When Buddy arrived at the beach he saw a boy swimming out by the entrance to the small cove. He was too far away to see how old he was, but Buddy's hopes soared. He sure would like to have some fellows around. That Linda was okay sometimes, but other times she was the biggest drip ever.

Sitting on the rocks, looking out to sea, was a man Buddy had never seen before. He went up to the stranger and said, "Hello. You're new here, aren't you? I'm Buddy —Buddy Barker. I live up the hill."

"My name's Carson," the man said, looking up at Buddy. "I'm glad to know you, Buddy."

"Glad to know you, too," Buddy said. He suddenly felt very foolish. This was the way little kids acted; rushing up to strangers and saying hello and stuff.

"You're an old-timer on the Island, I take it," Mr. Carson said.

"Yep. Been coming here every summer of my life. I don't remember all of them, of course."

"It seems like a nice, friendly place," Mr. Carson said.

"Oh, it is. That's why I came up to you like that. Everybody talks to everybody on Leete's Island. It's part of what Dad calls the LCOB—Leete Code of Behavior. Gosh, he even makes us be nice to people we don't like."

Mr. Carson suppressed a smile and said, "Well, I hope I'll be one of the people you talk to because you want to."

"Yeah, you look okay," Buddy said. "At least you didn't call me little boy and act like you wanted to pat me on the head. That's the worst kind. You gonna stay all summer?"

"My family will. I'm probably only going to be able to stay a couple of weeks," Mr. Carson said. "We've rented the Mason cottage. You must come see us," he added.

"Somebody always rents the Mason cottage," Buddy said. "They don't come anymore 'cause they're afraid somebody will drown Kenny. Accidentally on purpose," Buddy added.

Before Mr. Carson could inquire as to the reason why anyone might want to drown the hapless Kenny, Linda came around the big rock and Buddy called, "Hey, Linda, come meet Mr. Carson. He's new."

Mr. Carson stood up and offered Linda his hand. "How do you do, Linda?" he said graciously. "Won't you sit down and join us?"

Linda smiled and said, "I'm glad to meet you, Mr. Carson." It was the first time in her life a man had ever stood up for her and it was heady treatment.

The boy in the water was nearing shore and Mr. Carson called, "Ted, come here a minute, please."

Ted waved a hand and turned toward the rocks. "My son," Mr. Carson said and for a moment Linda's hopes reached cloud nine. Then the boy climbed from the water and Linda came back to earth. Ted was just about Buddy's age, she guessed.

Mr. Carson made the introductions and Ted and Buddy exchanged cautious, "Hi's."

"Buddy's an old-timer, Ted. Maybe he'll show you where it's safe to dive," Mr. Carson said.

"Sure. Let's go, Ted," Buddy said and they were gone.

"Ted was pretty angry with me because I wouldn't let him just plunge in," Mr. Carson explained. "He thinks walking in is sissy-stuff, but there's always a danger of hidden rocks in strange waters."

"We have our share," Linda said. "That whole side over there is a booby trap."

Moments passed, during which Linda stared at the water and wondered what to say to Mr. Carson.

"Quiet here, isn't it?" Mr. Carson said, reading her thoughts.

"Right now, but not for long," she answered. "You'd be surprised at the number of people living on the Island. There must be a hundred and fifty families. And sometimes, the beach looks as though they were all here at the same time."

"Buddy tells me you've been coming here for years," Mr. Carson said.

Linda nodded. It was difficult to make small talk with adults, even nice ones like Mr. Carson.

"Buddy also told me it's required that you be nice to everyone, but if you'd rather go sit alone and read your book, I won't take offense."

"Buddy told you that?" Linda said, sitting up straighter. "Every time I think he's growing up, he goes around saying stupid things."

"I'm sure he meant it in a nice way," Mr. Carson said.

"That's true. He'd hardly have said it if he thought you were one of the . . ." She paused, wondering how to express the thought.

". . . the miserable people?" Mr. Carson asked and Linda blushed. "That's all right. There are miserable people, Linda. I know," he added.

"Some of them don't turn out to be too bad," Linda said. "I mean, at first glance I thought I wouldn't like them at all, but after having to talk to them, I found they weren't so bad."

"And some were worse than you could imagine before-hand," Mr. Carson said. "Well, here comes the rest of the clan." He stood up and went to meet the three people coming around the rock.

Mrs. Carson, a tall, handsome woman with shining red hair, was in the lead; following her was a young man car-rying a small boy on his shoulders.

Mr. Carson lifted the younger boy off the older boy's shoulders and deposited him on the blanket. "Now, let's see what's proper in the line of introductions. Linda, this is my wife, my oldest son Barry, and my youngest, Ste-phen. Meet Linda Barker."

"How nice to meet you," Mrs. Carson said. Barry said, "Hi," and Stephen, with a four-year old's aplomb, ignored the situation. C544763 CO. SCHOOLS

"Is that Ted?" Mrs. Carson asked, pointing to a figure swimming fifty yards from shore.

"That's Ted," Mr. Carson answered. "He's with Linda's brother, Buddy, who's showing him all the hidden rocks and secrets of the cove."

"How's the water?" Barry asked Linda.

"I haven't been in yet," she said. "It's been slowly warm-ing up all week, but it was like ice last weekend."

"You've been here a whole week?" Mrs. Carson asked.

"Yes. We, that is, my brother and I, go to the Board-man School and it lets out after college graduation. We always manage to get here at least a week before every-one else."

"Your father teaches?" asked Mr. Carson.

"He's a professor of architecture at Columbia."

"How nice," Mrs. Carson said. Then she turned to her husband and said, "Walt, I've got a list of things we absolutely must have. Will you drive me into town later?"

"Of course," Mr. Carson answered. The talk between them turned to household chit-chat and finally Barry said, "I think I'll go in." He stood up, then as an after-thought, added, "Care to brave it?"

"Brave is the word," said Linda, wondering which was colder, the water or Barry's invitation. "It's funny, though. By August the water's so warm you feel like you're taking a bath."

"That's why I like the ocean. These coves heat up by the end of the summer." Barry shrugged as if to say, some things can't be helped.

Linda followed Barry to the edge of the rocks, noting his wide, well-muscled shoulders. Not the over-developed shoulders of a football player, more like tennis, she thought.

They swam out to the bell buoy, the limit allowed by common sense and parental decree. All the time they were in the water, Linda kept wondering what she should say to this boy. It was one thing to conjure up an imaginary boy and quite another to be faced with a real one. Funny, she thought, I never was able to think up a conversation even with my made-up boy. She contented herself with praying, Oh, please be nice.

When they came out of the water they found the Carsons had moved from the rocks to the beach and Steve was busily hunting for treasures. "Hope you don't mind, Linda," Mrs. Carson said. "We took the liberty of moving your things, too." Her smile was open and friendly, and

Linda appreciated the fact that Mrs. Carson had helped avoid a very difficult situation.

It would have been awkward to have had to pick up her own things and come to the beach as though following Barry; it would have been worse to return to her belongings and sit alone.

"Barry, will you keep an eye on Steve while your mother and I take a quick swim?"

"Sure thing," Barry answered.

Steve played at the edge of the water and made occasional trips to the blanket to deposit his treasures. The shells and pebbles piled up quickly but when he appeared with a dead horseshoe crab, Barry acted. "Oh, no you don't, fellow. Those things don't belong here."

"I want him," Steve said.

"Sorry, chief, no soap." Barry lifted the dead crab and threw him in the direction of the waste barrel.

Steve looked crushed and tears appeared in the corners of his eyes. "If you cry, Dad will make you go home," Barry threatened. The threat was effective: Steve turned off the tears and returned to collecting shells.

"Kids!" Barry exclaimed.

"He's sort of cute," Linda said. "That tear bit is a good trick."

"Yeah," Barry said and stretched out, his face toward the water so he could keep Steve in view.

"Do you have a boat?" Linda asked after a few minutes of desperate silence.

"Uh-huh. Steve, get away from there," Barry shouted and leaped to his feet to drag his brother from the edge of an over-hanging rock.

"Motor boat?" Linda asked when Barry returned.

"No, a sloop. Motors are kid stuff or for lazy adults," Barry said. "Mine's being shipped from our place in Jersey. It should be here the beginning of the week."

The way Barry clipped his sentences made Linda uneasy. It was becoming obvious that Barry did not have any intention of being stuck with a girl hanging around his neck all summer. His attitude seemed to indicate that he felt he was doing his share simply by being there.

Linda was seriously thinking of packing up and going home when Barry turned to her and said, "Sorry if I've been short. I've been concentrating on Steve and didn't really hear you. Here come Mom and Dad. My tour of duty is over."

"I didn't really say anything important," Linda said.

"What was that business about motor boats? I hope you're not one of the devoted owners who will be forever insulted at what I said."

"Gosh, no. It's just that my brother wants a motor for his pram," Linda said. "He's been pestering Dad all winter and spring about it."

"Think he'll get it?"

"No. When Dad says no, he means no. He takes a while making up his mind but once it's made up you might just as well try to move the Rock of Gibraltar."

"That's the way my Dad is. I keep reading these articles in magazines about parents being pushed around by their kids but it sure doesn't happen in our house. Maybe Mom and Dad don't read the articles," Barry said. He grinned at her and she realized that he was quite good looking; not handsome, but very satisfactory. She wondered if her nose were too red from the week in the sun and she hadn't even looked at her complexion since she'd left New York. And her hair must be a complete mess. What must he think?

"If I come up after supper would you take me on a tour of the Island?" Barry asked. "We should have at least an hour of daylight if I pick you up at seven."

"I'd love to," Linda said.

"Swell. Want to go in again?"

"No thanks. I promised Mom I'd be back early." Linda hoped the lie wouldn't count too heavily against her. She had things to do.

A STROLL AT DUSK

LINDA WALKED RAPIDLY UP the hill and broke into a run for the last twenty yards. She slammed the screen door and breathlessly said, "Hi, Mom. Mind if I wash my hair?" Without waiting for an answer, she moved to the kitchen and put two kettles on to boil. Then she dashed to the bedroom, found her manicure set, and returned to the porch where she set to work.

"Gosh, my nails are a mess. I haven't even looked at them all week. Are my tan Bermudas clean, Mom?"

"Linda, are you feeling well? Your face is so flushed I'm worried, and you talk as though you had a fever."

"I haven't felt better in years," Linda exclaimed. "Oh, there's my water."

Living in a cottage with no modern plumbing facilities was a challenge, especially to the fine art of washing one's hair in a basin, but Linda was an old hand at it. To the last basin of rinse water she added three drops of her perfume in order to smell lovely as well as look it.

Her hair washed, Linda gathered up the paraphernalia necessary for putting it up and sat on the front doorstep. She brushed the wet hair and watched the sunlight bounce

40

off it. "It's getting better, Mom," Linda called through the door.

"What's getting better?"

"My hair. It doesn't look so mousy. Mom, do you think blondes really do have more fun?"

"Linda Barker, I believe you're suffering from sunstroke. You haven't said one sensible word since you came back from the beach."

"Oh, but I have! I just neglected to tell you about Barry, that's all." Linda tossed off the last sentence casually, waiting for the exclamation she knew would follow it. She had not miscalculated.

"Barry who?" her mother said, getting up from her chair and coming to stand at the door.

"Barry Carson. His father is a dreamy looking man— like a British movie star. They rented the Mason place for the summer and I'm going to show him the Island after supper."

"I see," Mrs. Barker said, and the nice thing was she really did. She had known for some time that Linda was ready for the big step, and now that it was here, she was determined to remain aloof and offer no advice that was not asked for.

"Dad won't mind, will he?" Linda asked.

"I don't imagine so, dear. I'll talk to him when he comes in," Mrs. Barker said.

Linda was surprised and rather disappointed to discover she ate just as much at supper as usual. She had expected the excitement would leave her too bubbly for food.

Barry arrived promptly at seven and met the family with poise. Dad didn't ask any embarrassing questions or tell any of his not-so-funny jokes. In fact, it was a perfect beginning.

"We'll be back by dark," Linda said as they started toward the door.

"Better take a flashlight just in case," her father said.

"I've got one," Barry answered.

"Fine. Have a good time," Mr. Barker said, and winked at Linda behind Barry's back.

They started out walking rather stiffly since both of them knew Linda's father and mother were standing on the porch watching them. But once out of sight of the house it was all right.

After agreeing that yes, it was a nice night, Barry said, "Say, Linda, what's with your dog and cat? I've heard some odd names before—one woman at home calls her dog Percy which is the limit—but I really don't dig Baroque and Rococo."

"Nobody does who isn't up on architecture," Linda said. "Dad has a weird sense of humor and the names are his little joke. Baroque means exaggerated design or distorted shape, and Dad felt it fit the dog perfectly. Anyone can see poor Baroque is a sad mixture. His mother was less than a full-bred wirehaired terrier and his father was a dachshund which makes for that low-slung look he has. As for Rococo, that means superfluous ornamentation and Dad says there isn't anything more superfluous than a cat in a city apartment. So there we are."

"That's pretty clever," Barry said. "I like the kind of humor where you have to know something in order to see it's funny."

"Like *New Yorker* cartoons," Linda said.

"Exactly! Did you see that one with an Indian maid

and brave sitting under a tree and she was saying to him, 'I wouldn't marry you, Uncas, if you were the last of the Mohicans.' It wouldn't have been funny if I didn't know who Uncas was."

The discussion of humor took them down the hill and over the first side road. Linda mentally thanked her father for his careful cultivation of humor since she was holding her own with Barry.

A rabbit hopped across the road in front of them and off to the left a squirrel scampered up a tree. "This place is covered with small animals," Barry observed.

"All kinds. Rabbits, squirrels, birds, racoons, and of course, skunks. The racoons and skunks are great for tipping over the garbage pail so if no one told you, better put yours in a tree," Linda said.

"We found out the hard way," Barry said. "I had to clean up this morning. Thank goodness the pail wasn't full."

"They're pretty fresh. I guess they know that traps and guns aren't allowed on the Island so I think they've invited all their relatives from the mainland to live here too."

"It's nice they can feel safe," Barry said. "I don't see this business of shooting animals for fun or convenience."

He is nice, Linda thought. I just know Dad's going to like him. "We turn here," she said aloud. They followed a narrow road that twisted along until it came to the water. There was a jetty of rocks extending across the cove and on the far side of the water they could see a row of beach cottages.

At the end of the jetty nearest them was an old grey barge set high on rollers. There was a light showing through the porthole and Linda said, "Would you like to meet our one and only character?"

"Sure," agreed Barry.

Linda picked up a small pebble and tossed it against the boat, calling out, "Hey, Cap. Want some visitors?"

A lined, leathery face appeared at the porthole and looked out at them. "Why, Linda, of course I want visitors. Crawl up the stern and we'll sit out a bit."

Linda led the way around to the rope ladder that hung over the stern of the boat and she and Barry crawled up. "Cap could put in steps," Linda said softly to Barry, "but he thinks this is more in keeping with his motif."

Cap was there to lend Linda a hand as she reached deck level. "Good to see you, young lady. You get better looking every year. And I see you've got yourself a fellow. That's nice."

"Oh, Cap!" Linda said, but Barry merely grinned and she guessed he didn't mind. Of course, he'd probably had lots of girl friends and was used to this kind of remark. He may even have a steady back home, for all I know, she thought. The thought was too unpleasant to linger over.

"This is Barry Carson, Cap. His family's new here and I'm showing him the Island."

"Glad to meet you, young fellow. Sit yourselves down and I'll just get my pipe. Can't seem to keep track of it these days."

Cap, knowing he had star billing as the Island's only bonafide character, did his best to live up to his reputation. He wore a black patch over a perfectly good eye and his whiskers came down to his chest. His head, unlike his face, was completely bald, but since he never removed his cap until he was in bed, few people knew the secret. In

fact, he was called Cap because of the hat and not because
he was or had been a ship's captain.

"So, what d'you think of our Island?" Cap asked Barry.

"It's bigger than I thought. All these side roads cover a
lot of ground," Barry said.

"They do. Of course, nobody who sees the Island today
can really appreciate it. Before the '38 hurricane, it was
one of God's chosen spots. Never have gotten it clear in
my mind whether that hurricane meant the Lord had
given up on us."

"What was it like before the hurricane?" Barry asked,
knowing it was expected of him and also because he really
wanted to know.

"You been swimming yet?" Cap asked and Barry
nodded. "Well, guess you thought to yourself, this is a
mighty sorry beach. Well, didn't you?"

Barry squirmed on the nail keg and reluctantly admitted
he had thought the beach less than perfect.

"And so you should. It is a sorry beach. But it wasn't always that way. Next time you go down, you pay attention
to the set-up and you'll see what I'm talking about. That
rock formation that separates the coves is natural, anyone
can see that. But the rock wall separating the beach from
the road is man-made—and it sets on the best sand on the
Island. Had to do it, of course. Those rocks are breakers
in case of hurricanes and seems as if we get 'em more often these days. The old '38er took us all by surprise, but
nothing surprises us anymore."

Cap rambled on for twenty minutes telling Barry of the
old days when horses provided most of the transportation
and the fishing was good. "Reckon you don't know it, son,
but this used to be quite the place. There's an old aban-

doned quarry up the way, provided the granite for the base the Statue of Liberty sits on. Not many people know that, but it's true."

"You never told me that," Linda said. An abandoned quarry sounded like it might offer an adventure.

"Didn't I, now? Can't remember everything," Cap said. "Probably wouldn't have remembered it now, except I was up there the other day and it looked as though somebody had been messing around. Thought maybe you and Buddy had been doing a little exploring."

"I haven't," Linda said, "and I doubt if Buddy has. He usually tells all he knows, and he hasn't said a word about it."

With one part of her brain, Linda heard Cap say, "Seems to me I did show you my pictures of the Hindenburg when it passed over in '37, didn't I?"

She nodded as Barry said, "That's the one that exploded when it was about to land, if I'm not mistaken." Was she acquiring Buddy's active imagination? Did the use of the abandoned quarry have anything to do with the missing ABC mailbox? Or was it sheer coincidence?

The conversation flowed around her and Cap was answering Barry's question. "That's right, son. We were all pretty shook up about that, let me tell you."

"Cap, I promised we'd be back by dark so I guess we'd better go," Linda said.

"Best to keep your word," Cap agreed. "You come back again when you've got more time and I'll show you my scrapbooks. A regular history of the Island, I got in those pages."

"Thank you," Barry said. "We'll be back."

While a little light lingered in the clear spaces, the areas beneath the trees were already dark. The crickets were chirping away and off to the right came the sound of a bull-frog, sounding for all the world like Tubby the Tuba. Leaves crackled as the night animals began their roaming in search of food.

"This isn't such a bad place, after all," Barry said, and Linda knew her first reaction this afternoon had been correct. He hadn't wanted to come and was trying not to show it. "I just wonder, though, what you do around here for a whole summer. Doesn't it get kind of dull?"

"Loaf, mostly," Linda said. "It may not be exciting, but it can be tiring. And then, there's a movie in town, about eight miles away, if you want one. Mostly we read, play cards and Scrabble, and talk."

"No television?" Barry asked.

"No. Dad refuses to bring the set. He says the trouble with most people today is that they don't learn to live with themselves. If you always rely on external amusements your insides go to pot, especially the brain. We have a radio, but it's used only for the news and twice a week Buddy can listen to a ball game. Usually he doesn't bother. Somehow the outside world doesn't seem very important when you're here."

"I wonder if your Dad and mine are long lost brothers," Barry said. "They sure seem to be cut from the same piece of cloth."

"Well, don't tell my Dad. He thinks he's unique and we let him go on thinking so," Linda said.

Suddenly Barry said, "How old are you, Linda?"

For one swift moment Linda contemplated adding a year, then thought better of it. "Fifteen," she said. "Why?"

"Oh, no reason. You look about fifteen, but you talk older; with more sense than most girls I know."

What could she say to that? Nothing, so she wisely kept silent.

A DOG BARKS

MR. BABCOCK AND MR. CARSON were sitting with Linda's father on the Barker porch when Linda and Barry returned from their walk. Buddy was leaning on the table intently asking questions of Mr. Babcock. They came in as Mr. Babcock was saying, "You have to understand, Buddy, that Cairo is a fairly modern city in most sections. If a visitor doesn't stray off the main streets, it's rather like being in any other large city of the world."

"Did you stray? Did you run into Arabs with knives up their sleeves and beards covering scars? Things like that?"

"I'm afraid not," Mr. Babcock said, almost apologetically. "You do know, I hope, that beards are worn as a religious practice and not, as you so vividly put it, to cover up scars."

"Well, how about Communists? Did you meet any of them?"

"I suppose some of the people I met were Communists, but they didn't declare themselves, and since Communists don't look any different from other people I couldn't be at all sure. I'm really sorry, Buddy, but if you're trying to write a new television script about a poor professor becoming involved in international intrigue, you'll have to look elsewhere. I went to teach chemistry and that's what I did."

Buddy's face indicated clearly that Mr. Babcock's interpretation was correct and he felt more than a little disappointed at seeing his theory destroyed. "Oh, well," he sighed, and left the adults to continue their conversation.

"Want to play a game of Scrabble?" Linda asked.

"Sure," Barry said.

"In French, German, or English?" Linda asked.

"Good night! English," Barry replied rapidly. "Do you really have sets in French and German?" he asked as he put up the card table for Linda.

"We do. Dad made the sets himself. Said they would keep us on our toes. He's got a thing about languages. Fortunately, I'm pretty good at them, but poor Buddy isn't at all interested and that gets kind of tough on him after a while."

They settled down to play. Linda could hear her father explaining to Mr. Babcock and Mr. Carson the troubles he was running into with his airport design, and she smiled to herself. Dad always pretended he was a first class dope and she wondered why.

"I tell you," Mr. Barker was saying, "I had this magnificent idea about a round airport. The spokes of the wheel would be runways, all leading to the terminal building at the hub. The parking lot would be under the terminal and there wouldn't be anymore of these two-mile hikes from the car to the check-in desk. It was a great idea. Of course, I'd forgotten one small detail," he said sadly.

"You mean air currents, I take it," Mr. Carson said, playing along.

"Exactly. Head winds, tail winds, cross-currents. They seem to be fairly important to the fly boys," Mr. Barker said.

"They won't be when everything begins to take off vertically," Mr. Babcock observed. "You're just ahead of your time, Bill."

"That's what they say about all great men," Linda called out, and the men laughed.

"I train my children well, as you can see," Mr. Barker said.

Linda brought her attention back to the game. She was in a predicament. Not a vowel in her hand. Then Barry came to her rescue by building the word *cart*. She leaped to the *c* and added *w* and *m* to it.

"Hey, I'm not going to buy that," Barry exclaimed.

"Dad!" Linda called. "Tell Barry about *cwm*, will you?"

"So, you got Barry too? I hate to tell you, Barry, but she's right. She found the darn word in a book on Mount Everest and she's never let us forget it. It's some sort of mountaineering term, but it's valid."

"Pretty sneaky," Barry said.

"Oh, you think I'm sneaky! You should play with Mr. Babcock. He drags in all those nasty chemistry terms that no sensible person has ever heard of," Linda said.

"And you think *cwm* is a sensible word? A head doctor might like a look at you," Barry answered.

"Let's just say it's a terribly handy word when you haven't a vowel in your hand. *Ibex* is another good word for getting rid of the *x*. Pops up in crossword puzzles all the time. I collect the nice ones," she said.

"I see I'm dealing with a linguistic demon," Barry said. He added a wink and Linda knew he wasn't upset. That was good. She hated poor losers and especially boys who thought a girl should let them win. Barry obviously wasn't one of those.

They finished the game with Linda leading 140 to 125 and while Barry mixed the letters for the beginning of the second game, a sudden silence fell on the house. It lasted only a second or two and was broken by the sound of a dog barking wildly.

"That's Brownie," Mr. Babcock said. "Maybe I'd better run up and see him."

"I'll go," Buddy said, coming from out of nowhere and disappearing through the door before Mr. Babcock could move.

"Poor Brownie. We couldn't take him with us to Egypt and ever since we've been back he howls when we start out the door. I guess he doesn't feel he can trust us any more."

"Buddy will calm him down," Mr. Barker said. "He has quite a way with dogs."

"Buddy has certainly shot up," Mr. Babcock said.

"Yes, he's getting to be quite the boy," Mr. Barker admitted.

The barking stopped and the men returned to their talk about the political situation in the Far East. Linda and Barry played with a minimum of talk and no one seemed to notice that Buddy did not return.

The game over, Barry leaned back and said, "The quiet around here is amazing. We've always spent our summers in a resort town in New Jersey and the nights are filled with things to do, all of them noisy, I might add. I don't know if I'll be able to stand this all summer."

Linda had three separate reactions which followed in

rapid succession. Her first was anger and she wanted to say, if you don't like it here, why don't you go back to Jersey? The second reaction was fear: fear that she was part of the boredom Barry was feeling. The third reaction, and she admitted, the most realistic one, was understanding. Barry was feeling the way she had felt earlier in the week.

"You'll get enough noise on Monday to last you for weeks," Linda said. "Fourth of July is a big day here. There are races and a very loud band playing on and off—mostly off-key. And there's a huge picnic with everyone on the Island eating and drinking. Then the day gets finished off with a bang-up display of fireworks. Believe me, you'll be happy to hear the silence come after that."

Mr. Carson stood up and said, "Well, Barry, what say we amble on home? Church tomorrow and this fresh air is killing me."

Mr. Babcock and Mr. Barker laughed. "The first week is the hardest, Walt," Mr. Barker said. "We've turned in by ten every night this week and I'm just now beginning to function again."

"I'll be running along, too," Mr. Babcock said. "If my wife stops off, tell her to come home, will you, Bill?"

"I'll see you at the beach after lunch," Barry said quietly to Linda.

After the guests were out of earshot, Mr. Barker walked over to Linda and put his arm around her shoulders. "So, my little girl has a fellow."

"Oh, Dad!"

"I know, honey, you think I'm teasing. I'm not, Linda. I'm pleased, really, and Barry seems like a very nice boy."

Buddy returned at that moment and the intimacy be-

tween Linda and her father was broken by his headlong
dash into his bedroom. A minute later, Buddy called,
"Hey, Linda, could I see you for a sec?"

"What's the matter?" Linda asked. Buddy looked so
strange, his face flushed, yet giving the appearance of being pale. It frightened her to see him look so upset.

"Close the door, will you?" Linda did as Buddy re-
quested and came to sit down on the lower bunk next to
him.

"What happened?" she asked.

"There was a man! Linda, there was a man sneaking
around Mr. Babcock's house. That's what Brownie was
barking about. The man slipped around the corner of the
house into the woods when he heard me coming."

"Are you sure? It might have been the shadow of a tree
moving in the wind," Linda said.

"It wasn't any shadow! Linda, I'm telling you, there's
something going on with Mr. Babcock. Oh, I know you
think I'm cuckoo because I make up stories, but this isn't
one of them. Please believe me."

Linda hesitated, then said, "I believe you, Buddy. Did
you tell Mr. Babcock?"

"No," Buddy said, looking down at his feet.

"But why not? Don't you think he ought to know?"

"I . . . I thought about it, Linda, honest. And I was
sitting on the doorstep, planning to tell him when he came
home but then he came up the road with Mr. Carson and
I heard him say, 'Carson, do you expect me to put up with
this much longer?' And Mr. Carson said, 'You'll just have
to. This isn't kid stuff, Babcock.' So, you see, Linda, Mr.
Babcock knows about whatever is happening."

"It all seems so impossible," Linda said. Things like this

don't happen, except in books, she thought. She heard her mother come in the front door and begin to tell Dad about what a wonderful woman Mrs. Carson was and how much she had enjoyed her visit.

"I know what you're thinking," Buddy said. "The Carsons are nice people and they can't be mixed up in anything bad. But I'll bet this is only the beginning. I'll bet there will be fireworks before it's over." In spite of the shock he had received earlier, Buddy was back to enjoying himself. His eyes shone brightly and he looked happy.

"Buddy, you keep out of this—whatever it is!"

"I'm not looking for trouble," Buddy said. "I just happened to have been in the right spot tonight. Let's just say I'm the unofficial observer, huh? And Linda, I know you like Barry, but promise you won't say anything about this to him. It's funny business and Mr. Carson *is* involved."

"All right, I'll promise that if you promise not to go running into the middle of things." It was an easy promise to make. She had no intention of letting Barry think she was given to playing girl detective like Nancy Drew.

"Who, me?" Buddy asked innocently. "I'm just going to keep my eyes open and see what happens next. Because something will, you wait and see."

A DISTURBING

SUNDAY

Sunday began quietly enough. Breakfast was a pleasant occasion and the day promised to be fair and warm, but not muggy. Buddy had black circles under his eyes and he looked tired. Linda found it hard to be upset in the bright light of day, although she felt that this time Buddy was not indulging in imaginative flights.

The logical explanation was that Buddy had seen a burglar; logical for most situations, but not for Leete's Island where everyone felt safe. Had there ever been a robbery on the Island? If so, it was long ago because Linda could not recall having heard of one.

After breakfast, the family dressed for church. Linda put on her white, sleeveless piqué with the V neck. It showed off her tan beautifully, she thought, then suppressed the thought as being unworthy of a prospective churchgoer. She could not, however, repress the pleasure she felt at seeing her complexion clear of blemishes.

"Mom, my pimples have disappeared," Linda said as she emerged from the bedroom.

"I know," her mother answered. "You do look nice," she added.

56

"It must be the clean country air," Linda observed.

"I hate to say I told you so, but the air doesn't have a thing to do with it, Linda. If you think back over the last ten days, you haven't had a candy bar, a milk shake or a bottle of soda. That, my dear, is the difference."

"For gosh sakes! There's something to that diet business after all," Linda said.

"Now you know," her mother said. "When you get back home you'll have to decide whether you want to be lovely or succumb to the urge to be a member of the gang when someone says, let's all have a double malted."

Well, well, Linda thought. It works and without the help of wheat germ and yogurt, an odious mixture her friend Nancy's mother had tried quite unsuccessfully on poor Nan.

The natural reaction set in almost immediately; Linda could not keep from thinking about a hot fudge sundae with whipped cream, nuts, and a cherry on top. She hadn't wanted one until she had been reminded that she had not had one in ages. It was like reading a book about someone lost in the desert without water; the power of suggestion forced her to drink glass after glass of water. Problems, all the time problems, she thought.

"Let's go," her father announced and Linda shook off all thought of gooey temptations. Keeping her mind away from the subject was the only way to conquer it.

The church service was simple and comparatively short. Reverend Caldwell spoke on the theme of "Independent, yet ever dependent on God." Only once did Linda let her eyes wander and when she did she caught Barry looking at her from across the aisle. He gave her a wink and then turned his attention back to the sermon.

Reverend Caldwell stood at the door, shaking hands and exchanging greetings with the members of the congregation on their way out. He smiled broadly at Mr. Barker and said, "I heard you were back, Bill. Good to see you again."

"It's good to be back, Doctor. Our summers here are like a small piece of heaven on earth. Hope I'm not invading your territory with that thought," Mr. Barker said.

"Not at all, Bill," Dr. Caldwell said with a laugh. "Your family looks great. Linda's getting to be quite a lady, isn't she? And Buddy, you look as though you are going to be football material."

The exchange of pleasantries over, the Barker family moved on and out into the bright sunlight. By the time they reached the car, Buddy had his jacket off and his tie loosened. "This coat's getting awful tight under the arms, Mom," he said.

"You can't grow so fast, Buddy-boy," his father said. "I'll have to take two extra jobs to keep you dressed at this rate." The pride in his voice was unmistakable and Buddy glowed. It was good to be alive on such a day; beautiful weather and the knowledge that slowly but surely he was becoming a man pleased him.

The beach was crowded by the time Linda and Buddy arrived after lunch. Barry and Ted were sitting on the rocks and Barry called, "Over here, you two." Linda waved and, walking carefully so as to avoid crushing little fingers that were busily at work, made her way toward him.

"I saved six inches. That's all I could protect without calling out the National Guard," Barry said.

"I was telling your father yesterday that the quiet

wouldn't last. This is the beginning of the summer," Linda said.

"Been in yet?" Buddy asked Ted.

"No. I've still got ten minutes to wait. The Gestapo there is keeping check on me," Ted said, pointing to Barry.

"Listen, squirt, you can drown for all of me. But orders are orders," Barry replied.

"How about a walk around the cove?" Buddy asked. "I've got some time to kill and this sitting is for the birds."

"It's a good thing Mom or Dad aren't here to hear you say that," Linda said.

Buddy shrugged and she knew he was putting on a show for Ted. Letting him know that Buddy Barker was an all right guy.

"Do you ever get tired of having a kid brother?" Barry asked as Ted and Buddy disappeared around the bend.

"Just a little," Linda admitted. "He's getting better, though. Last year I wanted to strangle him continually."

"I know the feeling," Barry agreed.

After that exchange, there didn't seem to be anything else to say and they sat silently watching the other people. Finally Barry said, "My boat should arrive on Tuesday. If it's nice Wednesday, would you like to go for a sail?"

"Oh, I'd love to," Linda said. "I should warn you, though, I don't know a thing about sail boats. If you want help, you won't get it from me."

"You're the most honest girl I've ever met," Barry said thoughtfully. "You don't go around pretending to know more than you do like some I've known. How come?"

"I don't know," Linda said hesitantly. "Well, I guess I do, but it's hard to say without sounding silly. It's part of what Dad calls the Christian Ethic. Telling the truth can cause you a lot of trouble sometimes, but never more trouble than a lie. I've lived with that code all my life and it just seems natural," Linda said.

"You're a lucky girl," Barry said. "Well, how about a swim?" he asked, quickly dropping the subject. He dived into the water without waiting to see if she was behind him and swam out to the limit. Linda stood at the edge of the water and admired his form; the legs kicking eight kicks to one swing of an arm. It was a powerful racing form and Linda was glad she had paused to look. She'd have been left behind anyway so she might just as well enjoy the scene.

She slid easily into the water as Barry made his turn toward shore. Barry certainly was a boy of moods: all smiles and friendly one minute; all dark and almost antagonistic the next. Linda was floating on her back thinking about Barry's moods when he came up quietly behind her and grabbed her shoulders. She screamed.

"Hey, what's the matter?" he asked, swimming around to face her.

"I thought you were going to duck me and I'm terrified whenever anyone comes near me in the water. I'm sorry I screamed."

"But you're a top-rate swimmer, Linda. A little water shouldn't frighten you like that."

"I can't help it, Barry. It hasn't a thing to do with ability or common sense—I just get scared."

"Okay. I'll remember from now on," Barry said.

When they were back lying on the blanket, a twenty-four-foot, double-decked cabin cruiser slowly nosed its way in close to the shore. Two men came along the rocks behind Linda and Barry, dived in the water and swam to the cruiser. The men on deck helped the swimmers aboard, and the cruiser turned and slowly made its way back to the open water.

"You didn't tell me we had such high-class neighbors," Barry said. "That piece of ship must have cost at least thirty thousand dollars."

"I don't know who any of them are," Linda said. "I've never seen them before. There certainly seem to be a lot of strangers on the Island this year."

"All kinds! Like those Carsons, for example."

"Oh, Barry, don't growl. It's just that the Island is small and most of the people have been coming for years, so strangers are more noticeable. I didn't mean anything by it."

Barry seemed neither to accept nor reject her explanation. He was in another of his dark, silent moods, and Linda searched for the clue that would tell her why. What was there in what she had said about strangers that made Barry react this way? It was obvious from the beginning, she thought, that Barry had not wanted to come to the Island. Strong circumstances must have forced the issue, since it was clear that the Carsons had a cottage on the New Jersey shore and had been going there for years. Why this sudden break in habit?

Without quite knowing why, Linda asked, "Barry, what does your father do?"

"Do?" Barry said blankly.

"Yes, you know—work. He looks as though he ought to be a British movie star."

"Lots of women seem to think that. Mom says that's why he makes such a good lawyer. As long as there are women on the jury he can't lose, or so Mom says."

Neither the question nor the answer seemed very important until later in the afternoon. Barry was off swimming alone and Ted and Buddy were still verbally sparring, each trying to out-do the other in bragging about everything from their knowledge of airplanes to their prowess as athletes.

Having exhausted his own achievements, Buddy began to detail his father's abilities, describing in detail some of the buildings his father had designed. "And what does your father do?" Buddy asked.

"My father's got a real important job," Ted declared in loud tones. Then he stopped short and twisted the towel between his hands as though he had suddenly remembered something. "He's a lawyer and he helps people in trouble," Ted said.

Linda had been half listening as she dozed in the sun, and her ears caught the hesitancy in Ted's voice. He spoke the words as though it were a lesson he had learned by heart which had no meaning. Perhaps Buddy had been right about Mr. Carson being involved in the strange events which had already occurred.

Linda decided not to tell Buddy about her suspicions since he was already letting his imagination run away with him. She put the subject from her mind while helping her mother prepare supper that evening and didn't think of it again until more than twenty-four hours later.

"There's something wrong with the distribution of the work load around here," Mr. Barker said as he and Buddy loaded the car with the water jugs. "You women say you'll do the dishes while Buddy and I get the water and burn the papers, but doing the dishes consists mainly of throwing paper cups and plates into the basket for us to burn.

My father was right, we never should have given women the vote," he moaned.

"Poor Dad," Linda said, with deep sorrow in her voice. "I'll burn the papers for you. After all, you are getting on in years."

"Touché for our side," Mrs. Barker said.

"Buddy, let this be a lesson to you. Never bandy words with women. They always win," Mr. Barker said.

Rococo sat patiently at the door as Linda gathered up the trash can. He waited for her to open the door, then walked out in his leisurely fashion, spending considerable time on each of the three steps. "Getting to be a wild roamer, aren't you?" Linda said to him. "We'll be writing new words to the old song come September, Mom. 'How you gonna keep him down on Broadway after he's seen the farm?'"

"He is enjoying himself, isn't he?" Mrs. Barker said.

The papers burned, the water jugs filled, the Barker family settled down to a peaceful Sunday evening. Mr. Barker was working on the Double Crostic in the Sunday *Times* and muttering away to himself, as was his custom.

"Attention!" he said sternly. This was the signal for the rest of the family to stop whatever they were doing and prepare to provide reinforcements in the battle of the puzzle. "I want two words describing the next twelve months. Next year, coming year, and fiscal year do not fit. Nine letters," he said and sat back to wait.

"Year ahead?" Linda suggested after a long thinking process.

"You're a genius, a veritable genius, daughter," her father exclaimed. "I thank you."

"It was nothing, really nothing," Linda said turning

back to *Kidnapped* and the adventures of David Balfour. It was not David, however, that drew her on but Alan Breck. Now there was a man, she thought, and sighed aloud.

"Oh, this is awful," groaned Mrs. Barker a minute later. "The horrible woman writing this book says mullein is yellow and mine is most decidedly red. She must be wrong."

"Of course she's wrong, dear. Why don't you write your own book. You might call it something like 'Crisis in the Herb Garden or Who Dyed the Mullein?' Sounds rather like an Agatha Christie title, doesn't it?"

"Bill Barker, don't you get fresh with me," his wife said. "Did I suggest that you write a book on how to design a library without space for books when you did just that very thing?"

"Did you really, Dad?" Buddy asked.

"I did not," Mr. Barker asserted strongly. Then added, "Besides, it was only a preliminary plan."

It was typical Barker banter with everyone giving and everyone taking a little good natured kidding about his fallibilities. The sun disappeared behind the trees and the shadows on the porch deepened. Linda got up to put on a light and her mother said, "Hadn't you better call that miniature tiger of yours in before it gets any darker?"

"Gosh, I'd forgotten he'd gone out," Linda said. She went to the door and called, "Rococo." She repeated the call three times, peering through the dusk waiting to see him come galloping down the hill. She did not worry when he didn't come immediately since each day he expanded his roaming territory and took longer coming back.

Fifteen minutes later total darkness had descended and

Linda said, "I'll take the flashlight and look for him." She called once more from the steps and then walked up the hill with no results. She came back to the house and started toward the "Green Room," a Leete's Island euphemism for the out-house.

Just outside the square of light coming from the porch she saw Rococo. About six feet from him, she saw a second animal, all black but for one flash of white, and her mind registered one word: skunk. She screamed, "No, Rococo! Don't!" and flung herself at him, but he refused to be captured. She managed to get herself between the two animals and by shining the flashlight into Rococo's eyes, made him back toward the door. By this time her father and mother and Buddy were all out of the house and attempting to discover what the trouble was.

When Rococo was safely inside and Linda had calmed down she told them about the second animal. "Rococo's back was up and his ears were flat. I thought he was going to have a fight," she said.

"It must have been a racoon," Buddy said. "They have white faces, you know. If it had been a skunk, we'd have known it. And so would you, stupe. Boy, getting involved with a skunk is just about the dumbest thing anyone could do."

"You must really love that silly cat," her father said. There was a slight trace of confusion in his voice, as though he found it impossible for anyone to love a cat.

Rococo, completely oblivious of the conversation, lay stretched out on Linda's bed sound asleep. He'd had a busy day. Life in New York City was nothing like this.

STRANGERS AT THE PICNIC

THE SKY WAS CLOUDY ON THE morning of the Fourth but there was no threat of rain to disturb the feeling of gaiety that filled the air. Only Baroque was unhappy on Independence Day, for it was the one day in the year when he was not free to roam as he pleased. The fireworks sent him into a frenzy and he behaved quite as badly as Rococo did while riding in a car.

Baroque was let out for an hour's run at eight o'clock, and then locked in the house while the rest of the family went to town to see the parade.

"There's one good thing about owning that dog," Mr. Barker observed to his wife. "Our son does not pester us to violate the law and smuggle in fireworks for him to blow himself up with."

"You know, darling," Mrs. Barker said, "I shouldn't want word to get around, but I think you're a phony sometimes. You love poor Baroque and Rococo quite as much as the rest of us, but I promise not to tell on you—not that you fool anyone."

Mr. Barker winked at his wife and kissed her on the

cheek. "A loyal wife is what every man needs," he said lovingly.

The town was crowded and they had to walk almost a mile from where they parked the car to the center where the parade was held. The band music reached them long before they reached the parade and the *boom-boom* of the drums gave a lilt to their steps.

"Sound off, one-two," Buddy chanted and the family fell into step.

There was all the excitement of a small town parade; the balloon men shouted and little children either danced with delight because they had a balloon or cried with frustration because the decision had been, "No." In keeping with the times, there were balloons shaped like satellites and rockets as well as the usual round ones with painted faces and ears.

Linda looked around at the scene and was grateful that she had never liked candied apples or cotton candy. Her mental reserves were in full operation as she determined to resist all the sweet temptations the day would offer.

The most moving moment of the morning came when the bands assembled on the green and the flag was raised. The sound of the "Star Spangled Banner" sung by a surprisingly good soprano sent shivers up Linda's spine and she had to gulp hard to clear the lump in her throat. She wondered if others were as deeply moved by this simple ceremony as she, but it was such a personal experience, she dared not ask.

By the time they became unraveled from the massive traffic jam and returned to the Island, the picnic preparations were finished. The fire was burning with the white coals so necessary for a well-cooked hot dog or hamburger and the band was tuning up. The tables were spread and the people were arriving from all over the Island.

There was no need for any ice-breakers. Old friends found each other quickly and the talk grew to an uproar. Buddy had already decided he was going to keep an eye on Mr. Babcock and his suspicions were immediately aroused when he saw Mr. Babcock surrounded by three young men, all strangers to the Island.

"Hi, Mr. Babcock," Buddy said. "Did you go to the parade?"

"No, I'm afraid I'm too old for parades, Buddy. These young men," Mr. Babcock said, indicating the three gathered around him, "are former students of mine. They've dropped in for the day."

"Gosh, you look like the Notre Dame backfield," Buddy said.

"Thanks for the kind words," one of them replied. He was six-two and must weigh at least two hundred pounds, Buddy thought. His name was Jim and his friends were Hal and Mark, Buddy learned.

The talk turned back to college memories and when Jim said, "Say, do you remember Tubby Tompson, prof?" Buddy decided Mr. Babcock was in good hands and he said, "See you around," and moved off to find Ted. There would be a horseshoe game coming up and Buddy wanted to practice before the competition started.

The games started with the potato-sack race and Mr. Barker was determined to try. "Now, come on, honey. We haven't missed a year and we're not that old, yet," he said to his wife. "Besides, we almost won last year and I feel this is my year."

"Want to try?" Barry asked Linda.

"You don't know what you're asking for," she replied. "It's all down hill and most of the contestants end up rolling like Jack and Jill."

"Well, so long as I land on my head, there's no danger of damage," Barry said. He took her hand and added, "Let's show them how it's done."

Cap was in charge of tying the contestants into the sacks and he greeted Barry and Linda warmly as he had them step into the bag. Barry's right leg and Linda's left were tied securely together as the rules required.

"Don't tell anyone, but we have a natural advantage," Barry said. "You see, I'm left-handed, which also means I'm left-footed. You're a righty, so neither of us should be off balance."

"I didn't know people were footed as well as handed," Linda said with a laugh.

"Why sure. They're 'eyed' too. I learned that in biology last year," Barry said.

"Sometimes it bothers me how I lived to be seventy," Cap said, "without knowing all this stuff you young 'uns pick up nowadays. Here I am still trying to learn to trust riding in a car and you're probably planning on going to the moon. What a world I'm living in," he added with a touch of amazement in his voice.

Linda and Barry were one of the first couples to get into the potato-sack and she was grateful for the minutes it took before everyone else was ready. It was strangely pleasant to be this close to Barry and to feel his arm around her waist.

True to Linda's prediction, most of the contestants rolled their way to the finish line. She and Barry hopped across the line just a foot ahead of her father and mother.

"We won!" Linda shouted.

"And a fine mark of filial devotion," her father said from his prone position in the grass as he rested after the long haul. "You'd think young people would have more respect for age," he groaned.

"Now, would you really have wanted us to throw the race?" Barry asked. "You struck me as a man of integrity," he added with a glint in his eyes.

Mr. Barker turned to his wife and said, "I am going to stop talking to anyone under forty-five. I can no longer hold my own with this younger crew."

"Daddy, you're sweet and I love you," Linda said, leaning over to kiss him on the forehead. "Now, why don't you sit in the shade and I'll bring you a cold bottle of beer."

"That is the last straw!" Mr. Barker said, leaping to his feet. "I am not yet ready for the old people's home."

They all laughed together at Mr. Barker's histrionics and after her father and mother left, Linda thought Barry was going to say something, but he changed his mind. "Want a Coke?" he asked, as though needing to fill a gap in the conversation.

"Sure," Linda said, thinking, just one can't do too much harm.

They went for a Coke and came back with a hamburger, a hot dog, potato salad, baked beans, tossed green salad and a half-dozen sweet pickles piled high on a very unsteady paper plate.

"It's pure ambrosia and nectar," Barry said.

And you are my Apollo, Linda thought, but said nothing.

They were still recovering from the tremendous meal they had consumed when Cap took up his fiddle and called, "All right, now. Let's work off a little of that food."

"What's up?" Barry asked.

"It's square dancing time, pardner—are you game?"

"Well, I reckon I am," Barry drawled. "That is, if I can get up."

They warmed up with a Virginia Reel, moved on to the "Monkey Musk" and then swung into the "Wearing of the Green." Cap called the steps in his deep voice and no one had any trouble following him. Linda and Barry found themselves in a foursome with Jim, one of Mr. Babcock's former students. Linda might not have paid much attention to Jim but he had kept his jacket on in spite of the heat. During the "Monkey Musk" Linda was sure she saw the glint of a gun under Jim's jacket as he swung her round. It was a jolt and she heard few of Cap's words during the last number.

Cap was chanting, "You swing your corner lady, swing her high and swing her low. Now swing your partner all around you, swing her round and round. Then allemande left your corner girl, allemande your corner all. Now run back home and swing your own, the best gal in the town."

"And you are," Barry whispered to her.

Her mind a thousand miles away, she looked blankly at him and it was some time before she put Cap's last words and Barry's whisper together.

Oh, darn, she thought. He probably thinks I don't care and now what can I say?

She dropped to the grass and feigned exhaustion. "I've had it," she said, breathing heavily. "I should go into training for square dancing the way a boxer does for a big fight."

Barry wiped the perspiration from his face and sat down

beside her. "Is it permissible to get away for a swim or does LCOB dictate we stay close?" he asked.

"A swim would be wonderful," she said. "But let's wait until I'm sure I can make it to the beach, huh?"

Although it looked as though everyone who lived on the Island, past and present, was at the picnic, they found the beach crowded and had to settle for the rocks.

As Linda lay in the sun after the refreshing swim, she thought about the gun she thought she had seen. Should she mention it to Barry? Was she becoming a victim of Buddy's over-active imagination? She, who prided herself on being level-headed, was acting like a character in a very bad television show and she didn't like it.

"Are they worth a penny?" Barry asked.

"A dollar, at least," she said, grinning at him.

"Too expensive. I'll think my own," he answered.

"I was wondering," she said, improvising as she went, "how the world looks to Cap. I mean, here he was, born to a world of horses and now he's living in a world where Jules Verne isn't fiction any more."

"I know what you mean," Barry said. "I'll never forget the time I suddenly realized that my parents had not grown up looking at TV. And then I began to think about how really astounding it is to sit in my own living room and watch things happening all over the world. Do you know, they're working on delivering mail to homes by pneumatic tubes? The day of the postman is almost over."

"Imagine dreaming of growing up to be a postman and discovering when you're old enough to go to work that the job doesn't exist anymore," Linda said.

"What do you dream of being?" Barry asked.

"I used to think about being a teacher—I guess almost

everyone who likes school at all, has that dream, at least girls. But now I sort of think I want to be a librarian." She waited for Barry to snort or laugh and make a wise-crack, but he merely nodded and she went on. "I keep thinking that as long as there's any world worth living in at all, it will have books and I kind of want to work with them," she said.

"What made you think of libraries? Just because you read a lot?"

"Well, yes, that. But mostly I guess it's because some of the nicest adults I've met—outside of family friends—have been the librarians who helped me," she said.

"You know, I've never told anyone this, but, well I don't think you'll laugh." He hesitated, then went on with determination in his voice. Linda prepared herself to resist any temptation to smile that might arise. He sounded so serious about it all.

"When I was fourteen," Barry said, "I was really having more than my share of troubles. We'd moved around an awful lot and I was a freshman in a new high school where most of the kids knew each other and I was feeling pretty darn miserable. The guys didn't bother me so much, but the girls were a mystery to me. I couldn't talk to them, I stumbled over my big feet when I tried to dance—well, it was just awful."

Linda looked at the well developed, smoothly coordinated Barry and tried to picture him as an awkward adolescent—like the boys in her class, but Barry couldn't have been that bad, could he?

"I'd been in town about four months when one Saturday morning I went to the library. It wasn't my first trip, in fact I practically lived in the place. But this morning it was teeming rain and no one but a complete nut would be out, but there I was. The place was deserted and I was moping around, in and out of book stacks, and thinking about how there must be at least one book in the darn place that would make my life happier. The librarian came over and asked if I was having trouble. She meant in finding a book, I guess, but a few minutes later I was telling her every trouble I had. So, she hunted around and came up with six books, one on, quote, growing up, unquote, and the other five were those teenage girls' stories. She said if I read them, maybe I'd understand a little more about what makes girls tick. She said it was silly for boys to pretend that all girls' books were sissy stuff and why didn't I try. Well, she wrapped them all up in newspaper and I buried them under my rain coat. I guess I'd have dropped dead on the spot if someone had caught me with them.

"When I got home, I hid them in the bottom of the closet under my baseball equipment and didn't take them out except when I had the door locked. The funny thing about it is that it worked. I didn't go into school on Monday morning and take the place by storm or anything like that, but I had figured out that girls were people and that helped a lot."

"I'm glad you decided we belonged to the human race," Linda said, keeping her voice light.

"So am I," Barry said, looking down at her.

With a burst of confidence that surprised Linda far more than it surprised Barry, she said, "The summer isn't going to be so bad, after all, is it?"

"It begins to look tolerable," he said, wrinkling his nose at her.

FIREWORKS

Linda was happy she had not voiced her suspicion to Barry for when they returned, Jim was sitting on a rock in his shirt sleeves, talking to Mr. Babcock, Mr. Carson and Mr. Barker. He looked so friendly, with an open face that registered amusement freely, that Linda could no longer even pretend he was a sinister character.

The sun was in the west, suspended over the trees and the chaos had subsided. The adults were sitting, quietly talking, while the older children were at home changing from swim suits to play clothes. The younger children were probably taking naps so they would be awake to see the fireworks, Linda thought. That accounted for the fact that almost everyone in sight was a man, the mothers being at home until the children awoke.

Barry stretched out on the grass, his hands folded behind his head and gazed at the sky. He looked completely relaxed, Linda thought as she approached. She had put on clean Bermuda shorts and a fresh white blouse, and the clean clothes combined with the swim made her feel master of all she surveyed. She sat on the grass, near Barry, and enjoyed the momentary peace.

The peace did not last long. Buddy and Ted arrived carrying an old coffee container in which they held captive a small green snake.

"Isn't he a character?" Buddy asked Linda. "Look how he curls when I give him a little prod."

"We were looking for the little toads in your mother's garden so we could see if he'd eat one," Ted said. "But we didn't find any," he added with disappointment.

"Why, you miserable specimens of humanity," Barry said, sitting up with a jerk. "I ought to knock your head off, Ted, and I will if you don't take that poor snake over to the woods and set him free this minute."

"Aw, we aren't going to hurt him," Ted said.

"You're darn right you aren't. I'll set him free myself." Barry reached for the coffee can and since Buddy was holding it, the can was relinquished without a fight.

"Honestly, Buddy," Linda said as Barry walked off, "you act as though you were still six years old. That kind of stuff is for babies who don't know any better."

Neither Buddy nor Ted looked particularly chastened by the reprimands they had received, and went off to throw horseshoes as though the event had not occurred.

"Well, that's done," Barry said, returning with empty hands. "I'd expect that stuff from Steve, but Ted really ought to have out-grown it by now."

"I told Buddy the same thing," Linda said, "but it didn't appear to faze him in the least. I guess they get bored from hanging around."

"I suppose," Barry said and then lapsed into silence.

It was strange, Linda mused, that she had met Barry

just about fifty-two hours ago and now felt she had known him forever. She thought of the strained silence on Saturday and compared it with the comfortable silence now. Somehow he made her feel as though he simply accepted her as she was and she didn't have to pretend with him or attempt to prove herself.

"Barry," she said.

"Uh-huh."

"Before, we talked about what I wanted to do. What do you want to do with your life?"

Barry rolled over onto his side and picked a piece of grass to chew on. "Darned if I know, Linda. I read a biography of a famous lawyer like Clarence Darrow and I think that's the only job in the world. Then I read a book on the need for competent, honest policemen and I think that's what I want to do. I just don't know. It bothers me."

"You can hardly do both," Linda said. "I mean, either you want to send people to jail or keep them out."

"I don't think it's that simple," Barry said thoughtfully. "You see, a good lawyer is doing his share to see that the law is upheld and respected, only in a different way from the police. Do you see what I mean?"

"Yes," Linda said, dragging the word out so that it was half affirmative and half questioning. "I'll have to think about it," she added.

A few minutes later Cap sauntered over and joined them. "You don't mind a visit from an old codger, do you?" he said as he slowly lowered himself to the ground. "These things wear me out," he added with a sigh.

"Oh, you love them and you know it," Linda said.

"Of course I do. I didn't say I didn't like 'em, I said they tired me out. Difference there, Linda." He took out his pipe and puffed until the tobacco glowed red in the bowl of the pipe.

"Seems like we got more than our share of new faces this year," Cap said. "Those three big fellows look like policemen to me. I don't understand it but there's a funny feeling in the air."

"Why, those men are former students of Mr. Babcock's," Linda said.

"Yep. That's what he said." There was just a tinge of disbelief in Cap's voice and it unsettled Linda. It brought back to her all the small pieces of the puzzle: the missing mailbox, the shadowy figure at Mr. Babcock's house, the lack of conviction on Ted's part as to his father's job, and the gun she thought she had seen.

She glanced at Barry who looked quite uncomfortable and she wondered if he knew more than he was saying. Which side was his father on? And, more important, what were the sides? Could she . . . dare she ask?

"Golly, I never thought I'd be hungry again after that lunch, but I am. I think I'll pick up a few vittles. Want some, Linda?" Barry asked.

"I think I could manage to eat a little," she said and started to get up.

"I'll bring it back for you," Barry said. "Don't get up."

"Nice young man you got there," Cap said when Barry was out of range of his voice.

"I think so, too," Linda said.

She and Cap talked until Barry returned but neither went back to the subject of the strangers or the undefinable tension in the air.

"Well, I'll mosey along and get things ready for the big

blow," Cap said. "We did ourselves proud with the fire-crackers this year. Gonna be a lot of noise."

The sun disappeared behind the trees and a half hour later the Island was in darkness. The fire was burning itself out and the only other light was the flicker of matches as the men lit their cigarettes.

The fireworks display started with the simpler rockets and worked its way up to roman candles and pinwheels, and soon the sky over the Island was filled with red, pink, blue, and blinding white lights.

Despite her new-found sophistication, Linda found herself going "Ooh" and "Ah" as the spectacular display grew brighter and bigger and louder. When one unexpected bang made her jump, she reached for Barry's arm without thinking.

He gently released her grip and she thought she had gone too far in being friendly but he moved the freed arm to her shoulder and held her lightly. It was a comforting feeling.

The last firework went whirling through the sky, glowed for a moment and fizzled, falling to earth unexploded.

" 'This is the way the world ends, not with a bang, but a whimper,' " Barry quoted.

"I've heard that before," Linda said. "But I don't know where it comes from."

"T. S. Eliot," Barry said. "You'll get to him one of these days."

"Had enough noise?" Linda asked.

"For a while," Barry said. "It's been a nice day, Linda. I enjoyed it."

"Will I see you tomorrow at the beach?" she said.

"You bet." He tightened his grip on her shoulder for just a second and then said, "Good night, Linda."

She walked across the road to the cottage feeling as though she must be glowing far brighter than any mere fireworks. If there was a cloud above nine, she was on it.

Buddy was sitting on the living room couch comforting Baroque who was trembling as though about to come apart at the seams. Rococo lay on the coffee table with an imperturbable look in his eyes. His look seemed to say, well, I hope the nonsense is over with although I assure you, I found it quite dull.

"It's okay, fellow," Buddy said, giving Baroque a caress.

"Did you enjoy the fireworks?" Mrs. Barker asked Buddy.

"I didn't go," he said. "I stayed here with Baroque. The poor fellow needed company."

How strange boys are, Linda thought. Buddy was quite willing to capture a snake and try to feed it live toads, but he gave up the fireworks to stay with Baroque.

"That was nice of you," Mr. Barker said.

Buddy shrugged. "He's my dog," he said, and that explained everything.

"Hey, Bill," Mr. Babcock called through the screen door.

"Harry, come on in," Mr. Barker called.

"Won't stay a minute. Just wondered if you'd seen Brownie. We left him in the house, but he's gone."

"No, I haven't, Harry. If he's like our mutt, he's probably cowering in the darkest, deepest hole he could find."

"Yes, I guess that's it," Mr. Babcock said, but he didn't sound as though he believed his own words. "I hope nothing's happened to him."

"Oh, Harry, what could happen to Brownie?" Mrs.

Barker said. "He's an old hand on the Island. He'll show up."

Linda picked up the flashlight after Mr. Babcock had left, and said, "I'm going to the Green Room. I'll be back."

Linda had gotten just past the fireplace when she saw Brownie lying in the path ahead of her. She stumbled over a root as she rushed to him. It wasn't until she bent low that she saw the pool of blood under his head and she screamed.

The light wavered in her hand and she felt nauseous. For a moment everything whirled in front of her and she thought she was going to faint. "Dad, Dad," she called.

Mr. Barker came running up the path and Mrs. Barker and Buddy were close on his heels. "What's the matter, Linda? Are you hurt?" He reached her and put his arms around her. She shook violently and the tears were flowing down her cheeks.

"Oh, Dad," she moaned.

"What the . . ." Mr. Barker began, then his light rested on Brownie and he stopped short.

Mr. Barker let go of Linda and bent over Brownie. "Why, he's been shot," he said. "What . . . who . . . Oh, Lord, poor Harry and Sarah." Mr. Barker stood up. "Buddy, go ask Mr. Babcock to come here, will you? Don't tell him why. No, wait a minute. I'll go myself. Harry can't just be shown this without some warning."

"Those dirty rats!" Buddy said and no one chastised him for his choice of words this time. Stronger ones were in everyone's mind, even Mrs. Barker who was not given to harsh thoughts about anyone.

Mr. and Mrs. Babcock just stood and stared down at Brownie's inert body. Finally, Mr. Babcock said, "Buddy, would you go down and tell Mr. Carson I'd like to see him?"

"Sure thing."

As Buddy raced down the hill, Mr. Barker said, "Harry, what's Walt got to do with this?"

"I can't tell you that, Bill, at least not now. Maybe soon. But, this wasn't any accidental shooting."

"Come on, Linda, we'd better get back to the house," Mrs. Barker said. "I'll get an old blanket for you to wrap Brownie in, Sarah."

"Thank you, Mary," Sarah Babcock said between sobs. "Poor Brownie, poor innocent little dog," she said.

Mr. Babcock and Mr. Carson were left alone and the only words the Barkers heard was when Mr. Babcock raised his voice in anger and said, "This is a lot more than I bargained for, Carson!"

Mr. Carson's voice was low and his words did not carry through the night air. Only his tone came through, the voice of calm, considered, authority.

"Well, it looks like Leete's Island has a mystery," Mr. Barker observed.

Buddy opened his mouth to say, "Yeah, it was fun until this happened," then thought better of it. All he'd have to do is give his father one clue that he knew something was up and they'd have him on a leash tighter than any Baroque owned. Buddy clutched Baroque to his chest and whispered, "I love you, you mutt. And don't go getting yourself shot, you hear?"

Baroque looked up and licked Buddy's cheek.

MYSTERIOUS
MOVEMENTS

TUESDAY MORNING THEY BURIED Brownie. The Barkers, the Carsons and Mr. and Mrs. Babcock gathered together to see Brownie placed in the deep hole Barry had dug. It had been back-breaking work to dig through the rock filled soil and Barry had swung the pick with a violence that surprised Linda.

Mr. Babcock picked up the blanket in which Brownie was wrapped and placed him in the grave. There were tears on his face as he turned away to let Barry shovel the dirt back into the hole.

"I'll roll that big rock over the spot," Barry told Mr. Babcock. "That will keep the raccoons from digging the grave up."

"Thank you, Barry. You're a good boy," Mr. Babcock said.

It was an awkward situation with everyone standing around not knowing what to say or do. As they turned to go back to their respective cottages, Mr. Carson said, "I have to ask you not to talk about this. I can't offer an explanation now, but please, I beg you, don't talk about it."

"Anything you say, Walt," Mr. Barker said.

Barry rolled the large stone in place and there was nothing else to do but go back to the ordinary chores of the day. The water jugs needed filling, the kitchen floor had to be washed, and there were clothes to iron.

Linda tried to keep her mind off the subject as she sprinkled her blouses and shorts, but it was too vivid a picture for her to wipe away with one swish of the memory cloth.

"Mom, why does this seem so terrible? I keep trying to think, well he was only a dog, not a person, but it doesn't help," Linda said.

Her mother stopped mopping the kitchen floor and came out onto the porch. She looked tired and unhappy. "I suppose it's because animals, like small children, are so completely innocent, Linda. They're helpless in the world and they depend on the goodness of people for survival. When we fail an animal or a child, we've shown again that goodness isn't in all of us."

Linda nodded and her mother went back to the kitchen. As she spread a blouse out on the ironing board, Linda remembered the time when Rococo was six months old and they had left him alone in the house for longer than usual. When they came back, she found Roc had pulled every paper handkerchief from the box and ripped them to shreds all over her bedroom floor. She had been furious with him but when she had raised her hand to slap him, he had looked at her with such trust that she hadn't been able to hit him. She had settled for demonstrating her anger verbally and he had responded by hanging his head. But as she was picking up the scraps and saying angrily, "Oh, you!" Rococo had come and rubbed against her leg, purring wildly and all was forgiven. He was a dumb animal and that realization had led to new patience on her part.

After lunch she went down to the beach with Buddy, who talked all the way. He had spent his morning watching and listening to the goings-on between Mr. Carson and Mr. Babcock.

"Boy, Linda, I guess you don't think I'm so whacky anymore, huh?"

"No, I don't, but you don't have to look so happy about it. Being proved right isn't worth having Brownie dead," she said sharply.

"Gosh, I'm not happy, Linda. I'm excited, sure, but gee, you can't think I'd be that much of a louse, could you?"

"I guess not, Buddy. I'm sorry."

"Okay, just so we understand each other, as they say on TV. Things are really moving, Linda. Mrs. Babcock has been packed off to her mother's home in Boston. That fellow Jim who was at the picnic yesterday drove her to the station. And they're putting a huge spotlight on top of the Babcock cottage. I sure wish I knew what it's all about. But it must be serious."

"Whatever it is, I hope it gets over and done with soon. I wanted a little excitement this summer but this is more than I bargained for."

"Besides, now that you've hooked Barry, that's enough to keep you busy, huh?" Buddy said.

"Oh, get lost," Linda replied. "And don't you go around saying things like that in front of Barry or I'll wring your neck."

"Temper, temper," Buddy jeered. "Well, I'll see you around." He dashed off to join Ted, Barry, and Mr. Carson who were unloading a sixteen-foot sloop from a trailer.

Linda sat down on the rocks and watched them roll the boat onto logs and from there into the water. As soon as the boat hit the water, Mr. Carson left the boys. He looked harassed, Linda thought, as he strode toward his car.

Ted, Barry, and Buddy walked alongside the sloop, guiding it with their hands until she was out far enough to have missed the rocks. Then Barry climbed aboard and rowed the boat to the mooring post sticking out of the water some fifty yards from shore. He tied the boat securely, dropped the anchor for added safety, then swam back.

He flopped down beside Linda without saying a word, his face to the ground, and she understood that he was not willing to talk just yet.

"I'm going in for a dip. I'll be back," she said and moved off before he could answer. He needed to be alone and she didn't want him trying to be polite.

A while later he joined her in the water and they swam out to look the sloop over.

"She's beautiful," Linda said.

"I think so," Barry answered, "but then you always think your own true love is, or so I'm told. Have we still got that date for tomorrow?"

"If you're willing, I am."

By the time they were back on the beach and dried off, a flicker of life had returned to their conversation. Barry was animated as he talked about sailing and the joy of skimming over the water before the wind.

When the sailing talk ceased, Linda took courage and asked, "Barry, could I just ask one question? Is your father a policeman?"

"An investigator for the Customs Division," Barry answered. He waited for her to ask more questions but when she remained silent, he said, "Thanks for not asking, Linda. I don't know what's going on and even if I did I couldn't tell you."

"I know that, Barry. I just feel good to know your father's on the right side of this mess."

"So am I! Guys who go around shooting dogs are just about the lowest you can get. I didn't even know Brownie, but it made me sick."

"It took the wind out of Buddy's sails, that's for sure," Linda said. "He was having such fun playing detective but this has left a bad taste in his mouth."

"It always does, if you've got a grain of decency in you. Sometimes I wonder how Dad can be so darn happy with the world when he knows how many rotten people live in it. I think that's the thing people forget when they talk about how exciting a job it is. Sure, it's exciting if you don't mind worrying about whether you'll come home alive that night, and are able to keep the books balanced—the good people do out-number the bad, but there must be times when it's hard to remember that." Barry stopped suddenly, and looked at her. "Hey, it just dawned on me what you said before. How much has Buddy gotten onto?"

Linda sketched in the events that had led to a picture of mystery on the Island and when she ended, Barry said, "Well, you keep an eye on Buddy. This isn't kid stuff and he's just at the age when he probably thinks he's Sherlock Holmes and Perry Mason combined."

"Don't I know it," Linda said. "Are you feeling better about being here?" she added.

"Yes. I suppose you thought I was sulking because we

weren't in Jersey, but it wasn't that, Linda. This is the first time Dad ever had an assignment where he had to drag the family along and pretend to be just an average American citizen. It was the pretense that bothered me— and him, I might add. It isn't nice to sneak into people's good graces, even for a good cause, and deceit doesn't come easy to him. It was even worse when we found out how nice all you people were. It seemed like we were betraying you."

"Will you stay on even if this is cleared up soon?" Linda asked.

"You bet! We're settled for the summer and we'll stay even if Dad is called out on another case. That's the one bright spot in the thing."

"I'm glad about that," Linda said. She hoped she was not being too selfish in feeling happy at having met Barry even under such miserable circumstances. And then she added a silent prayer that the whole situation would be over soon and they could relax and enjoy the peace and quiet of the Island. It seemed centuries ago since that day in June when she had resented the Island's insular security and lack of action. Well, she thought, we never know when we wish for things how awful it can be to get them.

TIME OUT FOR FUN

LINDA PACKED THE LUNCH FOR the sailing trip and hummed happily as she fixed tuna fish sandwiches, hard-boiled four eggs, and rounded up a package of oatmeal cookies and six oranges. The oranges would quench their thirst better than anything else according to her father and she was willing to believe him.

"You'd better take my garden hat," her mother said. "You have a good tan but the salt water and sun can still add up to a nasty burn."

"You'd think I was going to Alaska the way the advice is pouring in," Linda said.

"Adequate preparation always insures a better time," her father said in his best classroom lecturing voice.

She wore dungarees and a white sweat shirt over her bathing suit and in the rush of last-minute running around, almost forgot to take a towel and bathing cap. She did hope they'd find a place to anchor and swim and she would be prepared.

Barry was at the beach ahead of her. He had made one trip out to the sloop, taking the sailbag and a jug of water with him. The sails were ready to be hoisted and Barry was eager to be off.

"Oh, I wanted to see you attach the sails," Linda said, as she settled herself in the stern as directed.

"The correct word is 'bending' them," Barry said. "You've got lots of time to learn—if you want to—but I thought the first trip should be just fun."

"Will you really teach me to sail?" Linda asked.

"I'll try. For now, let's settle for a few rules of the road. There's a life-preserver under the seat and you'd better wear it for a while, until we see how you do."

"But I can swim," Linda protested.

"I know you can swim, but if you get knocked overboard you may be unconscious and unable to swim until it's too late. I'm not being a fuss-pot, Linda. Too many people drown in boating accidents to take chances. The only other item you have to watch is the boom. They're just not kidding when they talk about lowering the boom on someone. It can knock you silly, so if I suddenly yell 'duck,' or 'watch it,' put your head down fast. Okay?"

"Aye, aye, captain," Linda said and saluted.

Barry checked to be sure the dinghy was securely tied to the mooring post, then dropped the centerboard and the main sail began to flap. The sloop came around to face into the wind while he hoisted the jib sheet and made it fast.

"We're off," he said, and the sloop began to move slowly. The wind was light and unsteady, but after they left the cove they picked up a strong moving breeze.

Once they were on a steady course, Barry turned to her and said, "You see, nothing like it. I sit here as relaxed as I'd be in an easy chair at home and the wind does all the work."

"And you called a motor boat a lazy man's toy!" Linda scoffed.

"You don't really want to hear that lecture, do you?" Barry said, smiling at her. "And if we lose our wind and have to row back you'll be sorry for those words, young lady. You do know how to row?"

"I have a feeling I shouldn't answer that question; I may live to regret it," Linda said.

They sailed for an hour along the coast, within sight of shore since Barry was still unfamiliar with the waters. He kept a sharp eye on the markings even though he seemed to be doing nothing. They talked about the houses on shore, the ones they liked, the ones they didn't, and they passed judgment on every boat that came their way. At the end of the hour Linda removed the life-preserver and Barry began to look for a spot to anchor.

They had a swim before lunch and the only problem arose when Linda found herself unable to climb aboard the circling sloop. The second try she almost made it, although the attempt just about cut her in two, only to fall back with a splash.

"Now, look," Barry said. "You put both hands on the edge and simultaneously push down with your arms and push up with your body." In one swift movement he was over the side of the boat and on the deck.

"This is like doing push-ups and I've never been able to do them," she groaned.

"Okay, land-lubber. I'll pull you aboard this time, but you'll have to learn. We'll practice before the next trip." He reached down and grasped her hands. "Any damage?" he asked as she collapsed on the seat.

"One scraped knee and a wounded pride," she said.

Barry dug into the small cabinet built in under the bow and brought out a first aid kit. He applied a generous helping of merthiolate on the scrape.

"You make me look like the last defender of the Alamo," she said. His concern and consideration for her welfare made it hard for her to jest but she did.

They ate lunch in silence and with gusto. The salt air, the swim, the joy of the day all added flavor to the food.

"Better not fall over-board now," Barry said. "I'd sink even with a preserver," he said, leaning back with the contentment of a well-fed man. The sloop rode easily on the small waves and the rocking plus the bright sun combined to give them both a sense of peace and well being.

"It's almost like being alone on earth," Linda said. "When I think of the noise of the City, it seems unreal."

"Linda?"

"Yes," she said.

"You really like your family, don't you?"

"Why sure! Don't you? I mean, like your family?"

"Gosh, yes," Barry said. "But, well, there aren't any buts about me liking my family. It's just that I haven't met many kids lately who do. Or at least admit they do. It's gripe, gripe, all the time."

"We're not all sweetness and light, you know. Dad has a wicked temper and sometimes he snaps and growls like a hungry mountain lion, but he loves us and we know it. That means a lot." She told him about the time she had called her father the meanest father in the world and how they had lived in something resembling cold war for a full week. "I guess we all have a time, some incident that makes or breaks a relationship," she said. "That was mine with Dad, and we've been friends ever since."

"You mean he showed you who was boss," Barry said with a wide smile.

"Well, yes, if you want to put it that way. He gave me a long lecture on how when he's the architect on a project he can't have the electrician deciding to put in wires any old place and the plumber installing pipes that lead nowhere. He said there can be only one person in charge unless you want chaos and he did not intend to have a chaotic family. He was quite willing to admit that we were individuals with our own clearly defined rights, but that he still retained a veto and would use it when he thought it best. It took a while, but I see his point—now."

Barry nodded. His eyes were closed and Linda took the opportunity to admire him unobserved.

"Back we go," he said, sitting up finally. "We don't want to lose our tide," he said as he pulled up anchor and let the sails out.

The return trip was without incident and they moored in the home cove at four o'clock. Barry quickly removed the sails and stored them in the sailbag which he placed in the dinghy. Then he held the dinghy close to the sloop and helped Linda aboard.

They found Ted and Buddy sitting on the rocks when they reached shore. "Mom says Linda can stay for supper," Ted said without preliminary talk.

"It was passed by the Barker Board of Trustees, too," Buddy added.

"I'd say you didn't have much choice, then," Barry said.

"I am delighted to accept the invitation," Linda replied.

"Since you two are here, suppose you help me carry the gear up to the house," Barry said. He parcelled out the water jug, his swimming paraphernalia and the basket in which Linda had packed the lunch.

"I told you we'd get drafted," Ted said to Buddy.

Barry lifted the sailbag to his shoulder and they trudged up the road, looking like castaways from *Robinson Crusoe*. It was a pleasant tiredness that Linda felt in spite of the stiffening that had settled in her scraped knee.

"I'll go up home and get dressed," Linda said. "I'll be right back."

She hadn't been in the Mason Cottage since the Masons had stopped coming, four years ago, and she was pleased with the way Mrs. Carson had turned it into an attractive, comfortable home.

"When the Masons had it," she told Mrs. Carson, "it looked like a monastic cell of some sort. Mrs. Mason was always grumbling about sand on the floor or dripping bathing suits. No wonder Kenny was such a miserable kid."

"Well, I admit, sand on the floor annoys me, too," Mrs. Carson said. "It's so hard to get it all onto the dust pan. There always seems to be a little left over to grind into the soles of my shoes."

"Didn't anyone tell you about your dirt-door?" Linda asked.

"Good heavens, what is a dirt-door?" Mrs. Carson asked.

Linda walked over to the table on the porch and bent down. "Here it is," she said. "See this small hole? You pull and up it comes." She demonstrated as she spoke and a twelve-by-twelve-inch section of the floor opened up like a trap door. "You sweep your dirt into it and it joins the rest of the dirt under the house. The wind blows under the house and spreads it out so you never get a pile."

"Well, I'll be doggoned," Mrs. Carson said. "This another of your father's gifts to harassed housewives?"

"Yes," Linda laughed. "He calls it his wife-saving device."

"I know one thing, dear," Mrs. Carson said to her husband, "if we ever get around to deciding where to build our dream house, Mr. Barker is going to design it."

"Agreed," Mr. Carson said.

"Maybe I can qualify for the agent's commission," Linda said.

There might be mystery and intrigue afoot on the Island, she thought during supper, but it was hard to believe, with all the goodnatured kidding and hearty laughter that filled the Carson house that evening.

As she and Buddy walked home at nine-thirty, a fine mist was coming in off the water. It would be a drizzle in another half hour.

"I have all the luck," Buddy said. "I got Dad to agree that I could sleep out tonight and now it's going to rain."

"Perhaps tomorrow night," Linda said. And then remembering Barry's warning, she added, "I think I'd like a night under the stars too. Will you mind?"

"No-o-o," Buddy said.

"Listen, squirt, if you're up to something, I'm going to be right at your side. Understand? I didn't ask you to convince me to play detective, but you did and now you're stuck with me."

"I'm not up to anything. For gosh sakes, do you think I'm a complete dope? I just thought I'd like to keep an eye on things and it's easier from outside."

"Okay. Just so you only look," Linda said.

NIGHT WATCH

By THURSDAY MORNING THE SKY had cleared and they had another beautiful day. Linda practiced trying to climb aboard the sloop while Barry gave her the first lesson in learning the vocabulary of sailing.

"Starboard is right, port, left," she repeated dutifully. "Bow is the front, stern is the rear."

The day was quiet but the tension in the air was becoming more noticeable. Mr. Carson made numerous trips between his cottage and Mr. Babcock's before he got in his car and drove off, looking worried. Mr. Babcock walked as though in a dream. He was lost without his wife, he told Mr. Barker. To have both her and Brownie gone was almost unbearable.

The most difficult part of the situation for Mr. Babcock was not being able to tell Mr. Barker what was going on. He was sworn not to discuss the matter and he didn't, but it was hard to avoid the issue.

It was a long day and by the time darkness set in Linda felt as though she had lived through a week. She tried to read but found her mind unable to absorb the words, and gave it up. Then she hunted up Rococo who lay sound asleep under the living room couch. She prodded him awake and tried to get him to play but the atmosphere had reached Roc too, and he gripped her arm with his two front paws and his teeth, bringing up his rear legs in a kicking motion.

"Hey, didn't anyone tell you eating people is wrong?" she said to Rococo, adding, "it's morally indefensible!" He glared at her. His ears went back and he crouched into what Linda recognized as his pouncing position. She backed away with Roc following and nipping at her ankles. "You'd think you were a dog, stupe. Now cut it out."

"You did wake him up, if I'm allowed an observation," her father said.

"I know, but he doesn't have to bite so hard," Linda said, displaying a badly scratched arm.

"You're beginning to look like a Civil War veteran. If I didn't know you better, I'd think you were still celebrating the centennial," her father answered.

"I'm just bored," Linda said.

"Bored? With your first real boy-friend and a mystery on the Island, you're bored? I'm surprised at you, Linda."

"Oh, Dad, I don't mean it that way. I guess I just want the thing to be over so we can go back to loafing."

"I agree with you whole-heartedly," Mrs. Barker said. "We've had quite enough of intrigue, as far as I'm concerned."

"While you two are feeling sorry for yourselves and your interrupted leisure, I suggest you give a thought to poor Harry. It is a great deal tougher on him than on any of the rest of us," Mr. Barker said.

It was beginning to get everyone, Linda realized. Her father's voice was sharper than usual and her mother wore a frown.

Linda played solitaire until nine-thirty when Buddy came in from playing with Ted. She hadn't won a single game and the frustration was building up.

"Boy, what a night for sleeping out," Buddy said. "The stars are out in force and there's a cool breeze."

"I've been wondering if it's such a good idea," Mr. Barker said. "Maybe you ought to wait until the mystery is solved."

"Oh, Dad! Nothing's going to happen to us. We're not involved in what's going on," Buddy protested.

"I'll keep my best big-sister eye on him," Linda said. "That is, for the forty or so seconds the eyes stay open once I crawl in. I'm exhausted." She yawned as though to emphasize her tiredness.

"All right, if Linda's sleeping out too, I'll shelve my protest. She's old enough to use her head," Mr. Barker said. "Where are you stretching out?" he asked Buddy.

"Same place as always, Dad. The clearing just this side of the fireplace."

"Sleep well," Mrs. Barker said, kissing them both good-night at the door.

They slept in dungarees and sweat shirts, and kept their socks on because the mornings were really cool on the Island. Outside, in the clearing, they spread their ponchos under the sleeping bags and crawled in. The bags were warm and they felt snug and content as they lay looking up at the stars.

"Don't go to sleep," Buddy whispered. "I want to take a look around after Mom and Dad turn in."

"Buddy, I don't think you ought to. I promised Dad, you know."

"Ah, don't be a spoil-sport, Linda. It can't hurt to look."

"And what do you expect to see?"

"Probably nothing," Buddy admitted. "But it seems more like a detective to at least look the land over. Besides, I don't know if you know it, but there are three agents posted within two hundred and fifty yards of Mr. Babcock's house. They've got some kind of signal system worked out so he can let them know if the guy they're waiting for shows up. I think it's probably by using the new spot light they installed the other day, but I'm not sure."

"How do you know all this?" Linda asked.

"I listen," Buddy said. "Shh, here comes Dad."

Mr. Barker passed them on his way to the Green Room and asked, "Awake over there?"

"Just barely," Buddy said. "It's great out here, Dad. You ought to try it."

"Thanks, Buddy, but I had all I want of sleeping on the ground during the war. I prefer innerspring mattresses and clean sheets."

Twenty minutes later the lights in the cottage went out and the stars provided the only light in the area. The leaves on the ground rustled as some unseen small animal made his way on his nightly forage for food, then all was still.

"Okay, let's go," Buddy whispered.

It was with genuine reluctance that Linda pulled herself from the warm sleeping bag out into the cool night air. It doesn't take long to get comfortable, she thought.

They walked as quietly as possible toward Mr. Babcock's cottage. At the edge of the woods, they stopped and looked around. Mr. Babcock was sitting on the porch with a book in his lap. He might appear completely relaxed to someone who didn't know him, but Linda recognized the sure sign that Mr. Babcock was worried: he was holding his glasses in his left hand and cleaning them with the thumb and forefinger of his right hand.

"They must be expecting things to bust wide open," Buddy said quietly. "He's sitting there like a decoy."

"Are you finished looking?" Linda whispered.

"Just about. How about one quick turn around the house? We'll stick to the woods so no one will see us." Buddy did not wait for an answer but moved off and Linda had no choice but to follow.

They had reached the rear of the house when the sound of a car coming up the hill froze them to the spot. It was strange how circumstances altered reactions, Linda thought. They must have heard ten thousand cars go up the hill in previous years and never given them a thought. The motor died away and they were getting ready to move on when the sound of heavy footsteps came from the left, just behind them.

"Under the house," Buddy whispered and grabbed Linda's arm and pulled her with him. Whoever was approaching was making enough noise to cover the little they were making.

They were out of sight by the time the footsteps reached the spot where they had been standing. They saw the feet walking around the house and then they heard the screen door slam.

Mr. Babcock's visitor had arrived.

MR. BABCOCK

HAS A VISITOR

BUDDY AND LINDA CROUCHED under the house trying not to breathe. The footsteps overhead resounded like thunder but the voices were muffled. Buddy put his mouth close to Linda's ear and whispered, "If we open the dirt-door an inch, we'll be able to hear."

Linda shook her head vigorously and whispered, "No. It's too dangerous. Do you want to get caught listening?"

"If the table's up, no one will know," Buddy replied.

He started to crawl toward the corner where the dirt-door was located. The space became increasingly smaller as they approached the door since the house was built on sloping ground. Linda followed him although her better judgment voted for staying where she was.

If the door squeaks when he moves it, I'll faint, Linda thought. She was trembling from head to toe and doubted that she would be able to stand should her very life depend on it.

The door opened easily and quietly and Buddy inserted a small chip of wood between it and the floor to keep it open. It was not possible to open the door far enough to be able to see, but the crack was sufficient to let them hear clearly.

"What have you done with my wife?" Mr. Babcock was saying. "If you've hurt her, Martin, I'll . . ."

"Now, slow down, professor," the man called Martin said. "Let's take things nice and easy and maybe we can work them out."

"All right, what do you want from me?" Mr. Babcock said.

"Why is it the brightest people always play dumb? I want my book back, professor. The hand-bound, gold-lettered volume of *War and Peace* which you were so kind as to carry off the ship for me."

"It . . . it isn't here," Mr. Babcock said.

Mr. Martin sighed as though the burdens of the world rested upon his shoulders. "I know it isn't here. If it was, we'd have found it Monday night when we searched the cottage while you were watching the fireworks. Incidentally, I'm sorry about the dog, but he was being a real pest, and my buddy lost his head."

Mr. Babcock started to say, "As a matter of fact," when the phone rang. He listened more than he talked and all Buddy and Linda heard him say was, "It will be all right, dear. I'll take care of it."

"Your wife?" Mr. Martin asked. Apparently Mr. Babcock answered with a nod because Mr. Martin went on. "Now you know that she's all right, we can talk business. Let's just say that she is our insurance policy, shall we? I get the book back, you get your wife. I'd call that a fair exchange."

"Get to the point," Mr. Babcock said. "What do you want me to do?"

"Professor, I've been following your trail for two full weeks and all of a sudden you're in a hurry. Suppose I make sure you understand me, before we get into details. Don't make up a story about leaving the book in your New York apartment. We've been through the place and it isn't there. It isn't here. Now, I hope you weren't foolish enough to run to the coppers because that would complicate the situation and might get the little lady hurt."

There was a pause and then Mr. Babcock spoke. His voice sounded strained and he spoke with precision. "Well, no, I didn't go to the authorities. You see, I, well, I have a reputation in academic circles, Mr. Martin, and I couldn't be at all sure I'd be believed. The truth of the matter is, I was scared of getting involved in a nasty situation."

Linda was so engrossed in the conversation that it was some minutes before she realized that Buddy was no longer at her side. She almost cried out but checked the impulse in time. Where had he gone?

"That's one of the things I counted on, Babcock, in case you were so unlucky as to discover the book and its contents. You self-righteous people are always more concerned with what others think of you than you are with what you think of yourselves."

"Why, you impudent, miserable . . ."

"Temper, Mr. Babcock. Remember, your wife is waiting. Now, where is the book?"

"I put it in my safety deposit box at the bank," Mr. Babcock said. "I thought that was the best place for it until I made a decision."

"An excellent move," Mr. Martin said. "An admirable move, in fact. You have talent, professor. Maybe now that you have made your first step towards compromising your principles, you'd like to take a second. There would be a place for you in our little organization, if you'd like. Make a lot more money than teaching a bunch of dumb kids."

"Blast it, Martin, I've had enough. I have to do business with you this time because you have me trapped, but I feel dirty being in the same room with you."

"You'd be great on the Perry Mason show, professor. We could call it 'The Case of the Indignant Professor.' Ever watch him? Not a bad show, is it?"

"Could we get on with the business at hand, please?" Mr. Babcock sounded tired and defeated and Linda wanted to stick her head through the door and comfort him.

Buddy reappeared magically and drew Linda aside. "What's up?"

"They're just getting to the point," Linda whispered. "Mr. Babcock has a book the other man wants, but why, I don't know."

"All right, professor, stay calm. Let's plot our *modus operandi*, as the wise boys call it. This bank of yours is in New York, I suppose?"

"Yes."

"Okay. Now, let's say it takes you three hours to drive down. I don't suppose you'll be doing much sleeping tonight so let's also assume you can be at the bank at nine when it opens tomorrow morning. Can you do that?"

"If necessary, yes," Mr. Babcock said.

"Where's the bank?"

"110th Street and Broadway," Mr. Babcock said.

"Okay. You go into the bank, get the book and stand on

the south-west corner of Broadway. I'll drive in to the curb, you hand the book through the open front right-hand window and your wife will get safely out the back door. Does that sound clear to you?"

"Yes, it's clear."

"Just one more item, professor, then we're finished. Don't sit up all night trying to figure out how to bring the coppers in on this. If anything goes wrong, and it won't if you do your stuff right, my pal and I will swear you were in on the deal from the beginning. The D.A. might not believe us, but enough people will to ruin you for good. Get me?"

"Oh, Lord, yes," Mr. Babcock said, the words sounding like Job's recognition of his fate.

"Well, then, we're all settled. I'll give the little woman your regards," Mr. Martin said. "Don't sleep too well," he added. "You wouldn't want to be late, would you?"

"Get out," Mr. Babcock said.

"I'm going, professor. It's been nice talking to you again. Let me know when you're taking another trip to Europe."

The door slammed above Linda's and Buddy's heads and it was suddenly very quiet except for the loud groan Mr. Babcock emitted.

"What do we do now?" Linda whispered.

"Stay put," Buddy said. "I have some thinking to do."

They heard the sound of a car motor starting up and heard it go speeding down the hill. Then silence fell again. Suddenly the darkness outside the house gave way to the light of a powerful spot light. Within thirty seconds after the light went on, Linda and Buddy heard the screen door open and Mr. Carson say, "What's up?"

"Martin just left," Mr. Babcock said.

"Is your wife all right?" Mr. Carson asked.

"Yes, she called while he was here." Mr. Babcock outlined briefly what Martin wanted him to do and then asked, "Can't you stop him, Walt?"

"We can try. Let me use your phone." Mr. Carson dialed swiftly and said, "Jim, a car went up the hill about twenty-thirty minutes ago. Did you get its make and license number?" Mr. Carson listened for a moment, then said, "All right, get here as fast as you can. We've got work to do."

"Did he get it?" Mr. Babcock asked.

"No, darn it. He says the only car he saw kept right on going and his orders were to stay out of sight unless the car was in your vicinity. That's true enough, but it makes things harder for us. Now we'll have to check every motel in the area without knowing exactly what we're looking for and hope they haven't checked out and moved on towards New York. What a mess I've made of this."

"I've got the license number if you want it," Buddy said, popping his head up through the dirt-door.

"Buddy! What in heaven's name are you doing there?" Mr. Babcock exclaimed.

"What do you know about all this?" Mr. Carson said sharply.

"A little more than you do," Buddy said with a grin. "Mr. Martin is driving a 1959 black Rambler station wagon with New York license 2Q-7294. He's also probably just about pulling off the road with a very flat tire. I stuck a nail in it."

"Well, I'll be a horn-tailed lizard," Mr. Babcock said.

The door opened and Jim appeared saying, "I'm sorry I missed him, chief."

"Don't worry about it. We've got to move fast. He is

driving a '59 Rambler station wagon, black, license number 2Q-7294, New York. Now, listen carefully. We can't pick him up because his pal has Mrs. Babcock and we can't risk his harming her. So this is what we do. He can only take one of three roads, to Guilford, Branford, or Moose Hill. I'd bet on Moose Hill since it leads to Route One where the motels are. You take that one. I'll send Hal and Mark in the other directions. He's probably changing a flat tire about now."

"How do you know that?" Jim asked.

"I haven't time to explain, so just believe me. If you find him, stop, offer to help, then drive on and call the others in. The chances of following him on that road are slim—not enough traffic—but see what you can do. If you locate the motel where he's staying, let me know. We'll use the bomb scare trick on them. Got it? Okay, check back as soon as you're on to him."

The door closed and Linda heard Mr. Carson dialing a number. He gave instructions to the two men he called Hal and Mark in the same precise tone he had talked to Jim. When he put the phone down, he walked across the room to within two feet of Buddy's head and bent down. "And now, young man, come out of there. I want to talk to you."

"Yes, sir," Buddy said meekly. "Do you want Linda too?"

"Good night! Is the whole Barker family under the house?" Mr. Babcock asked.

Linda and Buddy crawled out from under the house and made their way to the front door of the cottage. "Boy, we're probably in for it," Buddy said. "That Mr. Carson has a look in his eye."

"Just wait until Dad gets hold of us," Linda moaned.

Buddy stopped short and grabbed Linda's arm. "Listen, we didn't do anything wrong and they know a lot more about that Martin character than they would have without us, so don't you go apologizing."

"I'm not saying a word," Linda said, and opened the door.

CLOSING IN

"JUST LOOK AT YOU TWO," Mr. Carson said as Linda and Buddy came through the door.

Their blue jeans and sweat shirts were covered with particles of dead leaves, small sticks, dirt and cobwebs. Their faces were streaked where they had brushed the cobwebs off with very dirty hands.

The only white space shining through was Buddy's grin as he said, "Gosh, Linda, you're a mess."

"I doubt if you qualify as one of the ten best dressed men," Mr. Carson observed dryly.

Mr. Babcock rummaged around in three drawers before coming up with a clothesbrush. "Here, go clean each other off outside. I'll put on some water and find you a wash cloth and towel."

The cleaning up process took five minutes, although neither Buddy nor Linda particularly rushed. With their clothes half-way presentable and clean faces and hands, they sat stiffly on the edge of Mr. Babcock's living room couch.

"How about some cocoa?" Mr. Babcock asked.

"Swell," Buddy said.

"Would you like me to make it?" Linda asked.

"Thank you, Linda, but it gives me something to do," Mr. Babcock said. He had cleaned his glasses three times in the few minutes they had been sitting there and he paced up and down the cottage.

"It's going to turn out all right," Mr. Carson said. "Thanks to this young man," he added.

"I hope so, Walt. If anything happens to my wife, I'll . . ." The phone rang and Mr. Babcock froze in his pacing.

"You answer it, Harry. It should be my man, but just in case, you take it," Mr. Carson said.

"Hello. Yes, he's here." Mr. Babcock handed the phone to Mr. Carson who listened to his man reporting and finally said, "Good. Keep me posted. I'll call the local police and arrange for the next stage." He put his finger on the cut-off button to break the connection and turned to Mr. Babcock. "They picked him up about a quarter of a mile down Moose Hill Road. Jim says he hasn't heard such fancy swearing in years. The other men are closing in now and will station themselves along the road. The important point comes where he can only turn left or right. If we can keep him in line until he reaches the Post Road, we've got him. And even if we lose him, we've still got the license number and that's a big help."

Mr. Babcock, remembering the promised cocoa, turned and went into the kitchen. Linda and Buddy sat quietly as Mr. Carson continued his planning for the trap that was drawing closer to Mr. Martin at every second. He dialed again.

"Captain Walker, please. I see. This is Walter Carson

from the Customs Division. I talked to Captain Walker earlier this week about a job we're on, and we need a little help. Will you give me the Captain's home phone number? Thank you."

Mr. Carson broke the connection for a second and dialed again. As he spun the dial with one hand, he held the receiver between his shoulder and chin, leaving his left hand free to hunt for a cigarette. He found it and Linda got up to light it for him. "Thank you, Linda," he said softly and smiled at her. Leaning back in the chair waiting for Captain Walker to answer, he looked more like a stock broker calling the Wall Street Exchange than a man dedicated to fighting criminals.

"Captain Walker? Walt Carson here. Sorry if I disturbed you. We ran into a snag and need a little help." Mr. Carson quickly explained the basic situation to Captain Walker, then said, "We figure the bomb scare approach is our best bet under the circumstances. Remember, I outlined it for you when we talked. Swell. Will you handle the fire department for us? Remember, no sirens—that's important. These men are professionals and they'll run or fight if we give them the slightest hint. What's the number there? Fine, I'll call as soon as we know. Thanks, Captain."

Mr. Babcock delivered the steaming cocoa to Buddy and Linda and asked, "Coffee for you, Walt?"

"Thanks, Harry. That would be fine."

Linda took a drink of the cocoa and felt the warmth flowing through her. She realized suddenly that she was stiff; first from having crouched under the house and now from sitting as though afraid to breathe. She leaned back against the bolster and relaxed.

"Do you mind telling me what happens now?" Mr. Babcock asked as he handed the coffee to Mr. Carson.

"Yeah, what's with the fire department?" Buddy asked. "I never heard of catching crooks with a hose before."

"It's a comparatively simple device," Mr. Carson said. "Our basic problem in cases such as this, where the men we want are inside, is to get them outside without arousing their suspicions. It wouldn't matter too much if Mrs. Babcock weren't with them, but when they have an innocent person who can be used as a shield it's harder for us."

The phone rang and Mr. Babcock answered it as before. He handed it to Mr. Carson who listened, said, "It's all set with the local department. No, I won't come. Mrs. Babcock knows you and she is smart enough to take the hint when you give it to her. I don't think she will panic. Good luck, Jim."

He dialed the fire house and as he did, he said, "Some phone bill you'll have this month, Harry." He seemed so relaxed, so in control of the situation, that even Mr. Babcock allowed himself the luxury of a weak smile.

"Captain Walker? Carson. They're at the Shady Oaks Cabins. Know where it is? Fine. They're separate cabins as I was afraid they would be but if the fire truck is in clear sight, it shouldn't be hard. My men will handle any rough stuff. So, go ahead. And thanks a million."

There was a knock at the door and Linda heard her father saying, "Harry? Have you seen Linda and Buddy? They're supposed to be sleeping out but their sleeping bags are empty."

"Come on in and join the party," Mr. Carson called back. "Better get your wife, too. No sense in letting her worry about where you've all disappeared to."

Mr. Barker opened the door and stepped inside. He looked at Mr. Carson sitting comfortably by the phone; Mr. Babcock looking worried and twirling his eyeglasses; and then he let his eyes rest on Linda and Buddy, sitting on the sofa and drinking their cocoa.

"What are you two doing here?" Mr. Barker snapped. "This will be the last time you get permission to sleep out!"

"Gee, Dad, this is important stuff," Buddy said.

"Ha!" his father said sharply. "Your mother is frantic about you."

"Buddy's right, Bill," Mr. Babcock said. "Why don't you go get Mary and when you get back we'll fill you in on the details."

"Has everyone in this place gone stark, raving mad?" Mr. Barker asked, but he turned and left without waiting for an answer.

Mr. Carson waited until Mr. and Mrs. Barker arrived before he went on with his explanation. He had to wait while Mrs. Barker exclaimed over the condition of Buddy's and Linda's clothes and had satisfied herself that whatever was wrong, Linda and Buddy were in perfect health.

As Mr. Carson explained, Mr. Barker interrupted with, "Who is this Martin?"

"I'll fill in that part later," Mr. Carson said. "What interests us now is that Martin, his cohort, and Mrs. Babcock are at the Shady Oaks Cabins and it's my job to see that we capture those two without harming Mrs. Babcock in the process."

"But whatever is Sarah doing with two gangsters?" Mrs. Barker asked.

"That is something we don't know and won't know until she arrives and tells us," Mr. Carson said. "But it doesn't matter why or how she got there. What does matter is she is there and it's a dangerous position to be in."

"So tell us about the firemen," Buddy said, trying to bring Mr. Carson back to the point he had left them at some ten minutes before.

Mr. Carson looked at his watch. "Unless something has kept them, the fire department is arriving just about now. They'll go from cabin to cabin, pounding on the door and calling, 'Everybody out.' When they are asked why, they'll claim to have received a bomb scare call. Someone says there is a bomb planted in one of the drain pipes at Shady Oaks and they're there to locate it before it goes off."

"Suppose Martin won't come out?" Linda asked.

"That's always a possibility, of course, Linda. But we have two items working in our favor. The first is that there are just enough nuts in this world who do go around trying to blow the rest of us up to make the situation seem plausible. The second, and perhaps even more important, item is that the one thing Martin and his pal don't want to do is attract attention to themselves. And someone refusing to get out from under a bomb would be the cause of more than a little suspicion."

"Psychological considerations play a large part in your job, don't they?" Mr. Barker said.

"Yes, they do. We're always trying to figure one step ahead of these boys and it means understanding how they think and react. In a situation like this we're fairly sure, because no matter how evil Martin and his buddy are, they aren't insane. The ones who terrify us are the offbeats with a driving obsession which keeps them from seeing alternatives."

"What happens once you get them outside?" Buddy

asked. "How are you going to get Mrs. Babcock away from them?"

"Well, there will be a great deal of confusion and milling around and I expect Jim will walk up to Mrs. Babcock and say something like, 'Are you all right, ma'am? You look like you're going to faint.' And if she gets the idea, she'll collapse on the spot. By the time Martin and his pal recover their wits, my men will have handcuffs on them."

"Pretty smooth," Buddy observed with admiration in his voice.

There was a pause in the conversation and Mr. Barker said, "All this is very interesting, but will you kindly tell me what my son and daughter have to do with an apparently ruthless criminal?"

"Frankly, I haven't the foggiest notion," Mr. Carson said. "All I can tell you is that I was standing here kicking myself for being a fool and wishing I had the license number on Mr. Martin's car when Buddy's head popped up through the floor and produced the information. How and why he and Linda were there is still a mystery to me."

"Well, Buddy," Mr. Barker said, "what were you doing under Mr. Babcock's house?"

Buddy gulped hard and looked at Linda as if to say, well, help me out.

"Don't look at me. I just went along to keep an eye on you," she said.

The telephone rang and everyone in the room stiffened. Mr. Carson picked it up and said, "Yes?" He listened for a time while the others in the room sat tense and silent. "I see. Good work, Jim. I'll wait here for you." He hung up and turned to Mr. Babcock. "Relax, Harry, it's all over.

Jim is bringing Sarah home. She'll be here in a few minutes."

Mr. Babcock leaned forward and put his face in his hands. He said quietly, "Thank you," and no one had to question who it was he was thanking.

"Shall we save our explanations until morning?" Mr. Carson asked. "I should think it's been an exhausting evening for everyone."

"Oh, please," Linda said. "I've just got to know why that book was so important. I'll never be able to sleep if you don't tell us."

"Yes, you will," Mr. Carson said. "You're all invited to our place for a cookout tomorrow. We'll put all the pieces together then and see what our puzzle looks like."

"Gee whiz," Buddy said, but Mr. Carson's tone indicated that the subject was closed and there was nothing to do but say goodnight and leave.

"Pick up your sleeping bags and into the house with both of you," Mr. Barker said as they approached the cottage. "I'm going to have you within sight and hearing from now on."

Linda and Buddy did as they were told without protest. And despite the excitement of the evening and the curiosity which filled them, both were asleep within minutes after getting into bed.

EXPLANATIONS

THEY AWOKE SATURDAY MORN-
ing to a pouring rain. It was almost as though the heavens
were washing away the remains of any dirt Mr. Martin
might have left after his visit.

There was much running up and down the hill among
the Barker, Babcock and Carson cottages and finally it
was decided to have the lunch at the Barker's since their
house would accommodate the large group easily. Mrs.
Carson arrived early with the food and she and Mrs.
Barker worked together getting the party organized.

"I have the feeling food will play second fiddle today,
even with my hungry sons," Mrs. Carson said.

"I'm stunned by the whole situation," Mrs. Barker said.
"Apparently my two have been playing detective for
weeks and I never knew anything was wrong."

"Walt is as interested as you in discovering how they
became involved. The only thing he said to me when he
came in last night was, 'The case is closed, thanks to
Buddy Barker.' Then he shook his head and went to bed,"
Mrs. Carson said.

By noon everyone was assembled, and Mr. Carson had

no trouble getting the attention of the young people when he said, "I've always wanted to be able to stand before a group and explain a mystery the way Nero Wolfe or Perry Mason do, but I'm afraid this isn't my chance. This mystery comes in pieces, like a puzzle, and I think we'll begin at the beginning. Harry, will you tell us how this started?"

Mr. Babcock took off his glasses and rubbed them between his thumb and forefinger. "I met Mr. Martin on board ship on the way back from Cairo," he said slowly. "He told me he was a literary agent who toured Europe periodically searching for new authors and looking after the interests of his present authors. Since he was literate and well-versed in modern novels, I had no reason to doubt him. He was a very pleasant traveling companion and I must confess, I liked him. We played shuffleboard together, took dips in the pool, and he was always ready with a funny story, which he told exceptionally well."

"And he was a perfect gentleman to me," Mrs. Babcock added.

"He was, Sarah, and I'm quite sure he would have gotten away with his plot if I hadn't had my suspicions aroused. You see, that last afternoon before we docked, I saw Mr. Martin open my attaché case and place a book inside it. I couldn't for the world understand what he was up to."

"Why didn't you just go up to him and say, 'Look here, Mr. Martin, what's going on?'" Buddy asked. "That's what I'd have done."

"Human curiosity is a strange thing, Buddy," Mr. Babcock said. "After years in the classroom I have learned that the one way to insure not finding out why a person is acting oddly, is to ask him. One must observe the next step before a pattern begins to emerge. Or, to put it more plainly, I give them enough rope to hang themselves. That's what I was doing with Mr. Martin."

"But without any idea that Martin was a polished thug, not a classroom student," Mr. Carson observed.

"Well, yes, Walt. I'm not at all sure I'd have stood by if I had understood what was happening," Mr. Babcock said.

"What was happening?" Barry asked. "Why was the book so special?"

"Mr. Martin was engaged in smuggling contraband goods into the country," Mr. Babcock explained. "He had worked out a scheme by which he recruited innocent passengers to carry his goods through the Customs line and I was his victim this trip. The book in question was a hand-bound copy of *War and Peace*. It was an excellent choice since, as I think all of us here except Steve must know, it's one of the biggest novels ever written. Its bulk would not be suspect."

"Gee, I've read about things like that," Linda said. "They hollow out the inside and put the goods where the pages ought to be. But what would have happened if you had opened the book and looked at it?"

"Yeah, and what was inside it?" Buddy asked.

"To answer Linda's question first, I did look inside the book. There wasn't anything strange about it. All the pages were there, some 850 of them. Mr. Martin's group has come a long way from such crude methods. It was the cover that was hollow, and it was filled with cut jewels worth about one hundred thousand dollars."

"Wowee!" exclaimed Buddy.

"That would buy an awful lot of everything," Ted said.

"It would," Mr. Babcock agreed. "Of course, you realize I had no idea the jewels were there. I just knew that there must be something very odd about the book or my friend Martin would not have palmed it off on me. I got through Customs without anyone so much as handling the book. After all, a college professor is expected to be reading heavy books and it caused no discussion. I think Mr. Martin probably always picked professors for his unwitting accomplices for just that reason."

"That's a shrewd set-up," Barry said. "But, I'd have thought Martin would be waiting on the other side of the Customs fence to get his book back."

"I think that was Martin's plan, Barry," Mr. Babcock said. "However, something went wrong. I suppose Martin got in a slower-moving line and I was gone before he got through."

"If I may interrupt, Harry," Mr. Carson said, "I'm inclined to disagree. I think Mr. Martin was much too clever to have shown up immediately. I think his plan was to appear at your apartment in a day or two and ask if you had picked up his book by mistake. If you recall your conversations with him, I think you'll find that you told him where you lived without realizing it. In the confusion of returning from a year abroad, you might not even have glanced at your attaché case and you would find the book for the first time when he asked you to look for it. At least, that's my theory. But you go on with your part of the story."

"You may be right, Walt. Whatever his plan, we confused Mr. Martin by sending our trunks to the apartment while we took a train to see Mrs. Babcock's mother in Boston. It was there that I finally decided to take the book to the F.B.I. and see what they thought. It didn't take them long to find out the book was loaded. Since I was going back to New York and smuggling, unless the goods are stolen, isn't their business, they turned the case over to the New York office of the Customs Division and that's when Mr. Carson was called in to take over."

"Mr. Babcock," Linda said, "when I was under your house, Mr. Martin asked you if you had gone to the police and you told him no. Did you have any doubts about your decision?"

"No, Linda, not one. I have great faith that the innocent have nothing to fear from the law. Of course, I had to tell Martin a story and his kind of person is always willing to believe the worst of people. So when I told him I wanted to avoid the possibility of scandal, he accepted it."

"You lie pretty good," Buddy said.

"Buddy!" Mrs. Barker exclaimed.

"That's all right, Mary," Mr. Babcock said. "I did tell a whopping good story. I had the advantage of lying to a liar and for some reason, liars always think they are unique. They think lying is a carefully-developed art and one they alone have perfected." He leaned back in the chair and added, "Well, that's my part in this tale. I guess the rest is yours, Walt."

"Before I do any explaining, there are two things I want to say. First of all, I hope you all appreciate Harry's good sense in coming to us. We will never know how many others Martin used—and surely one or two of them must have noticed something odd, but they probably shrugged their shoulders and said 'Let someone else worry about it.' They're the people who make my job twice as tough.

"The second thing, and here I speak for my family as

well, is that we would like to apologize for being here under false pretenses. I know that Barry and Ted have been embarrassed by our false status but now that the job is over we're looking forward to being plain vacationers for the rest of the summer."

"Why, Walt, you were doing a job, and there isn't one of us who doesn't understand that," Mr. Barker said. "So forget it. I am interested in how you knew Martin would find his way here. Had he gotten Harry's address on board?"

"No, the only address Martin had was Harry's New York apartment. Now, we have to draw up a time-line for you to see what went wrong. On Wednesday, June 22nd, Harry and Sarah got off the ship in New York and took a train to Boston. On Friday, Martin showed up at the New York apartment and found a young couple living there. They were graduate students who had rented the apartment while the Babcocks were away. All they could tell Mr. Martin was that the Babcocks weren't due back until July 1st. They had no idea where the Babcocks were and neither did Martin."

"Boy, I bet he was worried," Buddy said.

"Maybe so, Buddy, but I think he just saw it as a minor delay. Which is all it would have been if Mr. Babcock hadn't gone to the F.B.I. He went on Monday, June 27th, and I arrived in Boston that night to talk to him. After listening to him, I realized that his summer plans made a lot of sense in the situation and we planned our approach for the Island. The open spaces and fewer people would make our lives easier than the city where the number of people coming and going are a nightmare for something like this." Mr. Carson went on to explain how the Babcocks had returned to the apartment, packed their summer clothes, and left the Island address with the superintendent who had orders to give it out if someone asked.

"Our initial plan was very simple—the simpler you keep plans the more likely they are to run smoothly. We expected Martin to show up here as a casual visitor and ask for the book. Mr. Babcock would tell him it was probably in New York and he would call the superintendent and have him send it out by mail. Then when Martin returned for the book, Harry would give it to him, signal us, and we'd pick Martin up at the foot of the hill with no fuss or bother. My mistake was in failing to realize that Martin was worried by then. He decided to get the book back without seeing Harry and that's when he went prowling Saturday night and again Monday during the fireworks. We knew what Martin looked like but we had no idea how many friends he had or what they looked like. That's when we realized that it would be best if Mrs. Babcock were removed from the scene."

"I wish you had told me what was going on," Mrs. Babcock said. "Of course, I knew something was wrong but it would have helped if you had told me it was Mr. Martin who was involved."

"That was our most serious mistake," Mr. Carson said. "It's hard to know when to tell someone and when to keep a secret. And obviously, we hadn't counted at all on Martin deciding Mrs. Babcock would provide him with adequate protection."

"How did he get you, Mrs. Babcock?" Buddy asked.

"Why, it was child's play," Mrs. Babcock said. "I was walking to the store to do a little shopping for Mother when I ran into Mr. Martin on the street. I greeted him like a long-lost friend and I guess he realized that if either of us knew anything, it wasn't I. So he offered to drive me to the store, and I got in the car."

"When Mrs. Babcock didn't return, her mother called Harry and we knew the chances were that Martin had kidnapped her," Mr. Carson said. "That meant altering our plan, since catching Martin was no longer enough. We staked out the men to watch for Martin's arrival, but we missed the car. Seems silly, but there it is. Which brings me to the most intriguing part of the story from my point of view. Just what were you doing under Mr. Babcock's house, Buddy?"

Buddy related the story as it had occurred, beginning with the missing mailbox and ending with, "Well, gee, when we heard someone coming we knew we couldn't just stand there, could we? The only place to go was under the house. Then I propped up the dirt-door and listened for a while. I figured that when crooks have a ransom victim, things are tougher so I thought maybe I'd better go get the license number of the car, just in case someone wanted it.

"You shouldn't feel too bad about missing the car, Mr. Carson," Buddy said. "There's a turnabout up behind the Hendrick's place and Mr. Martin had pulled in there. It's well hidden and there's a path from the Hendrick's down to Mr. Babcock's 'cause nobody uses the road much. After I had memorized the number, I dug around in my pocket and came up with a nail. I thought maybe if this character had to take time out to change a flat tire, you'd know how to snag him. Besides, I figured I owed him that much for what he did to Brownie."

"You have a talent for making the amazing seem matter-of-fact and the matter-of-fact seem amazing, Buddy," his father noted. "I will say, I'm not sorry you were prowling around last night, though I wouldn't want you to think I approve either."

"I get you, Dad," Buddy said. "But, honest, I wasn't out looking to be in the way or anything. I guess I just couldn't keep from having a look."

"That about wraps it up," Mr. Carson said. "There are a few loose ends that need tying up, but the worst is over. How about some food?"

THE SUMMER AHEAD

F OR THE REST OF THE WEEKEND talk centered around the events that had shattered the peace of the Island. By Monday they were pretty well talked out and the emphasis had shifted. Barry organized a morning course for Ted, Buddy and Linda in how to sail a boat and he proved a patient, but strict, master.

"I guess I don't want a motor boat after all," Buddy announced Tuesday evening at supper. "This sailing is okay." His attention shifted then to reading the ads in the newspaper of sailboats for sale.

Linda noticed her father made no comment at all about Buddy's new-found interest and she wondered if it meant that he approved.

On Wednesday, Mr. Carson returned to the Island after clearing up what he called the "loose ends of the case." He stopped by the Barker house after supper and told Buddy, "I've checked through and the only piece that doesn't fit is the missing mailbox. On my way back this afternoon I stopped by and asked Mr. Leete about it. He says some kids must have stolen it since it was found on a lawn about a mile down the road. It didn't have a thing to do with

126

the mystery except to get you started thinking something was wrong. And for that, I'm glad. You were a big help, Buddy, but don't let it ruin your perspective. You'll probably never run into another mystery in your life."

"That's okay with me, Mr. Carson," Buddy said. "I was scared silly once I found out it wasn't all in my head."

"Good boy. It takes real brains to know when to be frightened. Only the first class dopes make the mistake of thinking rashness is bravery," Mr. Carson said.

Linda watched her father nod his head in approval and she knew that he was very proud of Buddy. Even Linda could see that Buddy had taken a big step forward toward becoming an adult.

The big surprise came on Friday. At lunch, her father said, "I think I'll take the afternoon off and join you for a swim."

"Maybe I'll go along too," Mrs. Barker said. "The water must be warm enough for me by now."

There was nothing unusual about that and there didn't seem anything special when Mr. and Mrs. Babcock came down the hill to join them. As they reached the bend in the road they saw a truck with a sailboat on it. Two men were standing by to unload it as the group arrived.

The boat was a thirteen-and-a-half-foot sloop and the mahogany hull was glittering in the sunlight.

"Hey, isn't she a beauty?" Buddy exclaimed. "That's what Barry calls the blue-jay class, I bet."

"I'm glad you like it, Buddy. I hope you'll have many happy hours in it," Mr. Babcock said.

"Me?" Buddy's eyes grew round and he stood there with his mouth wide open.

"Catching flies, son?" his father asked, putting his arm casually around Buddy's shoulders.

"It's a gift, Buddy, for services rendered," Mr. Babcock said.

"Gosh, gee, thanks," Buddy said, stumbling over the words. "But you didn't have to do it and it must have cost a lot of money."

"Crime doesn't pay, as they say, but virtue does, Buddy. The government gives twenty-five per cent of the net value of smuggled goods turned in to it. Those jewels were worth one hundred thousand dollars, of which twenty-five thousand are mine. I think you deserve a share in the profits," Mr. Babcock said.

Buddy looked up at his father and said, "It's okay with you if I take it?"

"Yes, Buddy, it's okay with me."

"Wowee!"

"You present more of a problem, Linda," Mr. Babcock said. "We thought we'd wait and ask you what you might like."

"I don't want a thing, Mr. Babcock," Linda said. "I just went along for the ride."

"Besides," Buddy said, "she's got Barry and that's more than enough to keep her happy this summer."

"Brat!" she said, but she knew it was true and the blush told everyone else it was true. This summer wouldn't last nearly long enough, she thought.

3667
3935